THE DARK WOLF
SHAPES OF AUTUMN, BOOK FOUR

VERONICA BLADE

The Dark Wolf

Crush Publishing, Inc
Gardnerville, NV 89460
www.CrushPublishing.com

Crush Publishing, Inc name and logo are trademarks of Crush Publishing, Inc and are used only with its permission.

The places, characters and events portrayed in this book are fictitious. Any similarity to real persons, living or dead, is coincidental and not intended by author.

ISBN 978-0-9995994-0-2

Cover design and layout by Rose Nomura

Printed in the United States of America

THE DARK WOLF
SHAPES OF AUTUMN, BOOK FOUR

VERONICA BLADE

Crush
PUBLISHING

Gardnerville, Nevada

CHAPTER ONE
——— *Autumn* ———

THE LINCOLN NAVIGATOR slowed as we passed a weathered sign welcoming us to Genoa City, Nevada's oldest settlement. I craned my neck in hopes of a better view of an old Victorian house with a split-rail fence that lined the fringes of a wide sweep of land. The rusty wheelbarrow in front of an antique weapons shop, the weathered wood of the buildings, and everything I'd seen so far of this charming little town made me want this to be the place that hid the secret shape-shifter sanctuary we were looking for.

More than six hours had passed since we'd left Los Angeles and we'd crossed the Nevada border at least twenty minutes ago. I was more than ready for our trip to be over and couldn't wait to be fully vertical again.

Scooting away from Zack, I straightened my legs in an effort to get comfortable in the cramped third row seat. Okay, it wasn't that cramped. But six people in one car—Dathan in the driver's seat, Zack's dad Renzo in the front passenger side, and my parents Quentin and

Olivia, in the second row—made me crave a breather, no matter how roomy the luxury car might be.

The trip seemed especially drawn out with Dathan, the reluctant vampire king who we didn't always like. He'd saved our asses more than once back at his palace but I couldn't completely trust him. I wanted to. But while I'd grown to care about him, his arrogance and frequent dick moves grated on my nerves.

And he always kept us guessing.

"How much farther?" I asked Dathan. He'd been driving the entire time and was the only one privy to our destination, which I found odd. Up until a few weeks ago he'd been in slumber for seventy-five years, hiding from his duties as vampire king. How the hell did he know the whereabouts of a secret shape-shifter base? Cedric had been standing in for Dathan and ruling on his behalf—and still was. Maybe he'd relayed the information to Dathan.

Renzo straightened in the front passenger seat, making his dark head of hair visible. Glancing over his shoulder, he aimed a pair of gray eyes at me and shrugged. Sunshine streamed through the glass window, magnifying the fine scars on his face. "I have no clue where we're going," he said.

"Dathan," I said, making sure my voice easily carried past my parents in the middle seat and to his chestnut brown head. Vampires had superhuman hearing like other supernaturals, but that didn't mean Dathan was paying attention. "Giving us the deets anytime soon on the shape-shifter headquarters?"

"Almost there. I'll try Natasha again." Dathan's piercing blue eyes met mine in the rearview mirror as we cruised by what appeared to be the last store on the street before driving by a farm. The stench of cow pies snuck into the cab as he veered down a dirt road, past a sign warning us of private property. "All good. They'll be ready for us."

If he'd talked telepathically to Natasha the shape-shifter queen, that meant he'd already met her—before he'd gone into slumber. Which also meant Natasha had to be at least a hundred years old. The fact that she would allow him access into her top-secret shape-shifter compound also meant she trusted him. That was comforting.

I pointed ahead to a big ranch-style house situated just beyond crops that might've been corn. "Is it that big house on the left?"

Dathan scoffed and navigated the car through brush toward a mountain covered in trees and bushes. "Shape-shifters wouldn't live out in the open that way. But we're close."

"Thank God." My mom's head popped up and her big brown eyes peered through the windows at the landscape. She had spent most of the last several hours folded into my dad's tall lanky frame, the top of her nearly black head of hair contrasting against his sunny blond. She was the perfect height for snuggling with him. I used to envy her slight frame, hating that I'd taken after my dad and stood taller than most guys. I didn't have to worry about that with Zack. I could wear stilettos and he'd still have an inch or two on me.

My parents hadn't had much to say through the whole trip, even to me. But energy often swirled around them and I knew they were talking silently. I would've thought they'd be anxiously awaiting their reunion with other shape-shifters, maybe see some old friends.

And they'd barely acknowledged Zack or Renzo's existence since we left Los Angeles. Maybe their coldness had to do with Zack and Renzo being werewolves. But this wasn't a joyride or pleasure trip. Zack and Renzo had come with us to go to war against werewolves, their own species, on our behalf. That should have counted for something.

After our stint at the vampire palace where Zack and I had sought refuge from werewolves, we'd ended up in the middle of a werewolf-vampire war. When the dust settled and King Cedric and Dathan remained ruler of all vampires, Dathan had enlisted our help to take down the werewolf king's number one henchman, Ulric Vasilyev.

I had no clue why on earth Dathan thought a couple teenagers could help him bring down the most feared werewolf ever. Actually, he probably didn't. Most likely, he was more interested in what my parents and Renzo could contribute.

"I'm not sure about the safeguards they have in place." Dathan paused as he negotiated a bend in the road. "Since I'm a vampire, the shifters will be immediately suspicious of me. Autumn, you'll stand by my side to give me credibility. Quentin, you approach them first, so they don't catch werewolf scent straight away. Olivia, stay with him. Renzo and Zack, you go last."

Sounded like a plan. I imagined if the shape-shifters had several of their own supporting a vampire—my parents and me—they might be more hospitable. And Zack would be only a few feet from me during the introductions.

The road ahead turned to dirt lined with thick brush, and the only things visible on the other side of the windows were leaves and branches. The scent of moist earth and pine seeped into the car and made me crave a run. We hadn't morphed since last night and I was beginning to squirm in my seat. As a shape-shifter, I didn't need to morph half as bad as werewolves did. I bet Zack felt the urge a hell of a lot more than I did at the moment.

Dathan eased off the accelerator and I heard the whine of a motor, then a rock facade slid up directly in front of us. We passed under the fake rock wall and the hole sealed behind us, swathing us in pitch black. Dathan brought the Lincoln to a stop and switched on the headlights. We were closed in but still had enough space in what appeared to be a lift that would accommodate a pretty big truck.

A thump sounded above and metal clanked, causing all of us to flinch. Lights flashed and we descended. Although the car elevator was noisy, its existence in the boonies was pretty sophisticated. But

I'd expected no less from shape-shifters. They were weaker than werewolves and, if captured, used as slaves. But supposedly our intelligence far surpassed that of any other species. That's how we'd survived all these centuries.

"For being so smart, you'd think these shifters could make the entry process a little smoother," Dathan grumbled and the car swayed and jerked.

I swiveled to face Zack who hadn't said a word in over two hours. He stared at the back of the seat in front of us and chewed on his thumb, and I knew something was wrong. *Don't worry*, I told him silently, squeezing his other hand. *Dathan might have his own agenda, but he won't let anything happen to us, if that's what's bothering you. And after everyone realizes you're not like King Mortimer and other werewolves, they'll warm up to you and Renzo.*

The elevator motor slowed, the Lincoln bumped forward and then back again as the platform hit the bottom.

I know. Zack leaned over and brushed his lips against my cheek, and my insides warmed. *I miss my mom. I hardly spent any time with her after she came back as a vampire. If we make it through this and I go to war against my own kind, she might end up fighting with us and I don't want to lose her again.*

The lift door ahead slid up and Dathan eased the car forward. The walls of the tunnel were so close, he couldn't maneuver through the narrow passageway faster than a few miles per hour.

I worried about Zack's mom, Favianne, too. Thankfully, she was safe for now. *Kayla's training her for battle and she's getting stronger each day. Your mom will be fine.* I hoped Zack bought my wishful thinking.

If we lost the upcoming battle, Ulric would go after supernaturals like Favianne next—a new vampire mixing species with her werewolf husband, Renzo. Ulric wouldn't appreciate that anymore than he would tolerate Zack and me mixing. If we failed in stopping Ulric, he'd go after all of us. He already had the strength of the ancient ones, and drinking vampire blood had made him a more powerful force, probably the most dangerous werewolf in existence.

Any non-vampire supernaturals gradually went insane from consuming vampire blood for a long period of time. Ulric had developed a god complex, becoming sloppy as he killed and then drank from every vampire in his path. He not only hunted my shape-shifter parents, but also considered it his duty to destroy every rebel supernatural in existence. Me, for instance. Or Zack, a werewolf fraternizing with a shape-shifter.

As leader of Shape-shifter Werewolf Alliance Against Slavery and Tyranny, what we referred to as SWAAST, Zack's dad Renzo had already been fighting to gain equality for all species. Since he'd arranged to have Zack's mom changed into a vampire to save her life and they'd been reunited, Renzo had more reason to want Ulric neutralized and the werewolf king dethroned.

"Natasha just informed me of the reason for the extra racket during our entrance," Dathan hissed.

My mom straightened in her seat just in front of me, and leaned toward him. "Care to share?"

Dathan's knuckles stretched white around the steering wheel. "Natasha's security informed her that someone slipped in with us when the hatch to the tunnel opened."

My dad cursed, a rarity for him, and craned his neck to look around. Renzo squinted as he strained to see beyond the windows. Even with our heightened senses, we were challenged between the pitch black of the tunnel and the blind spots of the vehicle. Up ahead, the Lincoln's high beams shone on a metal door.

"Wait. How did they know someone snuck in with us when we didn't even realize it?" Zack asked, abruptly twisting his body to see outside the vehicle.

"Infrared showed seven sources of heat and there are only six of us." Dathan slowed, edging the Navigator forward until its bumper almost rested against a huge metal door.

"And they're only just now telling us?" Renzo growled.

"The heat source stayed on the roof. Naturally the security guy assumed the seventh person was inside with us. When the seventh body disappeared, he alerted Natasha right away." Dathan mumbled something under his breath. "We might have to wait while they beef up security. They want to make sure that the intruder doesn't slip inside the compound with us."

Renzo's gaze focused beyond the car, scanning the darkness. "So they saw the heat source actually separate from our car and move through the tunnel?"

"Yes," Dathan replied, rapidly tapping his fingertips on the console as we waited for the wide metal door to slide open.

"If they're tracking him by infrared, they know the exact location of the intruder, yes?" My dad's words should have been calming but the churning in my stomach told me we were both about to be grossly disappointed.

"The intruder moved off the roof and within seconds all traces of heat disappeared. They lost the feed from the infrared cameras." Dathan shifted and the leather of the seat creaked.

Which meant that no one would see if anything happened to us. Every single muscle in my body tensed, and silence filled the cab for the next few very long seconds.

The immense metal slabs divided and a bright light momentarily blinded us. Dathan rolled the car forward and the doors slammed shut behind us. In an instant, about ten heavily armed men all dressed in black and camouflage circled us, some of their gazes focused on the entrance as others checked under and around our car.

As if satisfied no danger was present, the men backed up then bowed as a blond woman approached, flanked by another group of guards.

The woman, Natasha I assumed, stopped and jabbed a finger toward an empty parking space. She wore black cargo pants with combat boots and a basic black tee. She stood tall, but slightly shorter than me, with a slender frame. The ends of her golden blond ponytail grazed the nape of her neck as she watched us with vivid blue eyes. Judging by the lack of wrinkles around her delicate features, she couldn't be more than thirty by human standards. But her prior connection with Dathan told me she'd graduated high school decades ago, not years.

"Zack, Renzo, don't forget to lag behind." Dathan parked the Navigator alongside a row of several other cars, then killed the engine and climbed out. Remembering he wanted me by his side, I tapped on my mom's shoulder and she opened the door. "Autumn, remember to stay with me."

Since we suspected an intruder in the vicinity, sticking close to Dathan wouldn't be a problem for me.

"Natasha," Dathan said. A secret look passed between them, then she gave him a small nod before turning to my parents who'd just exited the car. Her eyes widened and she beamed, launching toward my dad. After a brief moment, she threw an arm around my mom and squeezed them both. "Why didn't you tell me you were coming?"

I had no idea my mom or dad had ties to any shape-shifters. Obviously they'd have to know their own queen, right? But how did the queen know them so well?

"When Dathan mentioned teaming up with other

shape-shifters, we had no idea you were involved." My dad hugged her tighter. "We certainly wouldn't have wanted to bring you into this mess and put you in danger."

"Oh, please. If someone is fighting Ulric or King Mortimer, I want in," Natasha scoffed, then offered a cocky grin. "Besides, you can't very well bring shape-shifters into a war and not include their queen."

"Unfortunately, you're in whether we like it or not," my mom grumbled, hugging Natasha for what seemed an eternity.

Dathan shifted his weight forward. "Considering we just let someone into the tunnel and no one knows where he is, we should probably get on with the introductions and get out of the parking area."

"I agree, Your Majesty. I'd feel better if you were inside and not so exposed," one of the men said. He had a German accent and his wavy shoulder-length blond hair made me think of Thor.

Natasha gave an almost imperceptible roll of her eyes. "Trapped in that tunnel and no way to get to us, Egon. He can't dig through the titanium shell of our structure."

"I prefer to be prepared for anything, Your Majesty," Egon returned with a respectful bow.

A scent wafted to me and I zeroed in on the guards. Egon smelled of werewolf. Knowing a werewolf held a position close to the shape-shifter queen eased the apprehension that had become more intense with each passing moment in the closed off mountain where we couldn't easily get away.

I glanced at Zack whose eyes were darting around in paranoia. Although Renzo was more subtle about being on high alert, he was turning in slow circles trying to see everything all at once.

"We'll catch up later." Natasha released my parents. "You'd better get your luggage."

Some of the guards hovered around us, their eyes scanning the vicinity while we each grabbed our belongings. With our duffel bags slung over our shoulders, we moved toward the door in unison. Except Egon the werewolf, who hung back for one last check around the structure.

"This level is exclusively for parking and storage." Natasha maintained a brisk pace across the solidly packed dirt floor of the parking lot.

Massive beams supported the high ceilings and wood cabinets covering the back wall, each with a padlock. "How would you get in and out if the lift breaks down and you can't access the tunnel?"

"In an emergency, we drive out." Her head tilted toward the other end of the long expanse of space where a green exit sign lit up a panel the size of a garage door. "But we prefer to enter and exit some distance from our base, otherwise we risk revealing our location with tire marks."

"How is that exit reinforced?" Dathan asked, staying close to Natasha and her guards.

"The six-inch steel door seals airtight," she answered without breaking her stride. "If you don't have a code, there's an emergency lever which can only be opened from the inside. And unless it's done properly through my security people, an alarm will sound."

"So there's no way that guy is getting out of the tunnel?" I asked.

"He doesn't have the access code and no one here will help him. Even if he somehow got through, there are over fifty of us," she said with a shrug. "That said, until we figure out how to neutralize him, we won't be leaving. We weren't planning on going anywhere for at least a few days anyway."

Once we were past another steel door and it shut behind us, a lock clicked and Natasha breathed a sigh of relief. We'd ended up in a small space that looked to be a holding room of sorts.

"There," Natasha said. "Safe. Whoever got in isn't getting into the parking structure, much less out of the tunnel. And certainly not in here. I'll be fine," she told the werewolf guard. He nodded at the men, then everyone disbanded and disappeared through the next door, except him and three others.

Natasha twisted, hitching a pinky at the four remaining men as she named them off, starting with the werewolf. "This is Egon, Rakin, Kieran and Haji." On the last guard, she ended up face-to-face with Dathan and her eyes narrowed. "Been a while."

He flashed a slow grin as his gaze swept the length of her. "Too long?"

"Not nearly." Natasha scrunched up her nose, then refocused on my parents. "Why don't you introduce me to your friends?"

My mom gestured to me. "This is our daughter. Autumn, this is Natasha, a dear old friend."

Natasha blinked slowly, studying me a beat before speaking. "It's wonderful to meet you." Her mouth parted like she wanted to say more and I wondered what the rest of us were missing. Definitely a story there. Fat chance of getting anything out of my secretive, tight-lipped parents.

"Nice to meet you too." I offered a smile, squashing the urge to hunt down that dog who'd slipped into the tunnel with us.

"Don't worry," Natasha told me. "Even if he got out of the tunnel, he's not getting past that door. Our security is the finest anywhere."

"Good to know." But I'd heard that line before. At the vampire palace, the enemy had found a way to attack King Cedric in his own chamber. He'd almost been killed. I'd stick to the harsh reality I'd learned to hate—always be prepared for the worst.

She switched to Dathan. "I'm curious how you became aligned with werewolves and shape-shifters."

"These werewolves are Autumn's friends. Her friends became mine when she agreed to marry me," Dathan said, slowing down on the last two words. "I took the time to get to know them and I've seen for myself that they're trustworthy." He draped an arm around my waist and shot Zack a glance over his shoulder. *Just go along with it and I'll explain later*, he told Zack and me telepathically.

His fiancée? Dathan had to be kidding.

Unfortunately, I was dealing with Dathan which meant he was likely deadly serious and I had to proceed with caution until he let us in on his secret plan. Whatever he was up to, I probably wouldn't like it.

CHAPTER TWO
—— Zack ——

A GROWL CAUGHT in my throat. Autumn's gaze whipped to me but she didn't object or try to push Dathan away, which made me think she'd heard what he'd told me.

Damn right he'd explain. *Autumn's fiancé? What the hell?* I demanded.

Natasha studied Autumn a moment, then aimed a look at Dathan. "She's awfully young for someone your age. Midlife crisis?" she asked wryly.

"You wish." Dathan hit her with a smug, lopsided grin then tilted his head toward my dad. "This is Renzo. He leads SWAAST."

"Nice to finally meet you," Renzo told Natasha, extending a hand.

She accepted, shook and released his hand. "The honor is mine. There are many grateful shape-shifters here who I'm certain would love to thank you personally."

"I'd be happy to speak with them." Renzo flicked a thumb at me. "This is my son, Zack."

"You are very welcome here, all of you," Natasha said, and flashed me a warm smile before drifting to Autumn, her gaze lingering there an instant too long. Her fascination with my girlfriend was the least of my concerns after the stunt Dathan had just pulled. "I'll show you around the compound, then get you settled into your quarters."

Keep it down, Zack. I sense your mutinous thoughts from here, Dathan told me silently as we all moved to follow Natasha and her men. First Dathan and Autumn, then her parents. Renzo and I trailed at the back while I fumed at Dathan for ignoring my question.

He threaded his fingers through Autumn's as they walked and I wanted to pummel him. Thankfully, she had a physical connection so she could hear what I said to him. *Dathan, what the hell are you doing?*

Natasha led us through another door and we trailed after her up a shadowed steel stairwell. "Sleeping quarters are on the next floor up. We'll skip that for now and fast forward to the top level."

Just when I wanted to grind my teeth in frustration, Dathan finally answered my question from what seemed like a lifetime ago.

I'm the only vampire in a camp full of shape-shifters and a sprinkling of wolves, he said. *I need a way to anchor myself to the community, other than Natasha who clearly isn't overjoyed to see me; something that gives them a reason to trust me. Being engaged to Autumn was the best way. I didn't warn either of you because I knew you'd object and it wasn't up for debate.*

Sometimes you're such an ass, Dathan, Autumn said, her eyes ablaze. *I can't believe you ambushed us that way.*

You'll thank me later, my furry friends. For now, let's pay attention to Natasha. We need to know our way around this place. Dathan released Autumn's hand while still staying close to her.

Amusement tugged the edges of Autumn's mouth. *Don't worry, I can break off our engagement anytime.*

True. But something told me that regardless of Dathan's dick move, he had a plan up his sleeve. And, unfortunately for me, it was probably brilliant. *Let's roll with it for now.*

Seething from fury, I willed the corners of my mouth up in an attempt to appear friendly. I didn't need the shape-shifters sensing my hostility and thinking it was directed at them. I couldn't risk anything compromising our mission.

Any idea why Dathan said he was engaged to Autumn? My dad asked as he walked alongside me.

Not yet. I commanded my hands to relax and not to curl into fists as we continued up the stairs. *Gives him credibility with Natasha's people. But I'm pretty sure I still want to kill him.*

I'll help you.

Appreciate it, Dad. I wanted to be amused at his attempt at humor—even though Renzo probably wasn't joking—but I couldn't make my mouth do anything other than tighten.

Damn Dathan! If his plan helped to get rid of

Ulric and King Mortimer though, I'd go along with it. Once we beat them, less would be standing between Autumn and me.

Until I knew eternity with Autumn was in the realm of possibility, I could never tell her how deeply I loved her. The less she invested in me, the less devastated she'd be if we separated. I frequently fantasized about a new werewolf king in place, and werewolves' prejudice for shape-shifters dying along with King Mortimer. Maybe discrimination would always exist to a greater or lesser degree, but I hoped socializing outside my species wouldn't always be illegal. And then I could finally get it all out and tell Autumn the truth.

I had a long ways to go before that fantasy became a reality and now Dathan had made the situation more difficult and awkward. Trusting him had been a bad idea.

Natural light illuminated the first landing. *If you try to share a room with Autumn, I'll kill you*, I told Dathan. I'd be extremely challenged against the world's oldest and most powerful vampire, but I couldn't let him think he could take any of this lightly.

Relax, Zack. If I wanted your girl, you'd already be dead. He glanced over his shoulder for the briefest instant. *Listen to your father and keep your emotions in check. Don't ruin your chance at freedom because you can't... what's the modern expression? Suck it up?*

Dathan continued up the stairs toward the third floor, leaving me staring after him. What pissed me off more was that he was right; I needed to stay focused on our mission.

But why did he have to be such a douche about it? One minute he saved our lives, and shared his blood with us—which apparently he never did, not even for his own kind—and the next moment he sabotaged our happiness. I was beginning to really dislike him.

Shoes clanged on metal steps as Natasha neared the landing. "The third floor is for work, training and social activities. But since we're overcrowded at the moment, a portion of the common areas are being used for additional sleeping."

"I thought we were underground, but you have windows," Autumn said, craning her neck to peer over her shoulder. "How do you keep humans from figuring out there's a whole village inside the mountain?"

Natasha paused before a door and glanced toward the sunshine streaming into the stairwell. "The windows have a special film that blends in with its surroundings on the outside while allowing us to see out. We've planted poison oak near the windows and posted No Trespassing warnings everywhere. Should anyone ignore those, which is rare, the motion sensors alert us when anyone ventures too close."

"Clever." Dathan grabbed Autumn's hand again, making me wish she had kept quiet and not drawn attention to herself. "Solid security, sugar. Same as our palace."

Our palace? *Sugar*? And how long had it taken to come up with that pet name? Now I *really* wanted to murder Dathan.

Natasha rolled her eyes at Dathan. "Laying it on a little thick, don't you think?"

"Jealous?" Dathan's mouth curved up on one side.

Natasha's blue irises deepened before she spun around to carry on with the tour.

I didn't want to imagine what had happened between those two in the past. At least one of them still had feelings for the other, obviously, even if those emotions were negative. I just hoped their unfinished business would work in my favor and Dathan would give up the pretense with Autumn soon.

"Each level is over twelve thousand square feet," Natasha continued. "Due to the sheer size, stairwells are located at all four corners of the building on every floor, as well as the center."

Egon opened the door and Natasha slipped through. With the rest of the men behind her, she made a sharp left. My attention drifted from the unpolished plywood floor under my feet to the textured walls as I filled my lungs with air, searching for normal building smells like plastic, paint or other chemicals. The place had been built all green, all natural, and they'd kept it plain—no baseboards or crown moldings adorning the plain white walls.

"Your Majesty," two men both said, bowing their heads as they passed her.

"Gentleman," she returned. They disappeared into the security room and Natasha resumed her job as our tour guide. "This is where we monitor the exterior and all possible entry points." She jerked her head to our left.

The way they addressed her reminded me of her position. Despite my fury with Dathan, I appreciated that we rated a personal tour by the queen herself.

Renzo nudged my shoulder. *When you've been around as long as Dathan has, you find entertainment in the strangest ways. Don't let him get to you.*

I was more worried about Dathan getting to Autumn than him getting to me. *I'll try.*

"Since we house shape-shifters of all ages from around the world, as well as werewolves, we have a nondenominational chapel. There's also a theater which is equipped with a commercial-size screen and reclining chairs," she said before hanging a right. "That's where we've been keeping the overflow. But you won't be sleeping there."

"I should hope not," Dathan hissed. "I assumed we'd have more suitable arrangements."

"My, we think a lot of ourselves." Natasha raised one eyebrow at him, then carried on with the tour. She took us through another door which opened into a huge room with rows of tables. "This is the cafeteria."

We'd eaten shortly before we arrived but it was always good to know where to find the food.

"You'll be dining over there with me." She indicated the corner where a wide open door lead to a private room, a skylight showering sunlight onto a table that sat eight. "I usually eat around five, before everyone else. Sean insists it's easier to protect me with fewer people around."

Upon exiting the cafeteria, we encountered

two shape-shifters, a statuesque black woman with razorblade cheekbones and hair clipped extremely close to her scalp, and a bulky man with short light brown hair. Natasha stopped for them and the rest of us bottlenecked behind her.

"Ah, here are the two I depend upon most. Sean and Yvonne, meet our guests Quentin, Olivia, Renzo, Autumn, Zack and Dathan." Natasha flicked an index finger as she named off each of us. Standing in the back, I struggled to keep a straight face when Natasha said Dathan's name too softly. As if by barely saying his name out loud, he didn't really exist. I inclined my head in hello while the rest of them did the how-do-you-do's.

Natasha agreed to meet with them later and she ushered us forward, stopping in front of a sign that read 'Research.' "This side of the floor is devoted to research and manufacturing."

"Working on any projects you can talk about? Flying cars or anything like that?" Autumn asked.

Natasha sent a curt nod to an approaching group—one of them a female werewolf. She sidestepped so they could get by, and her mouth arched up. "Better. It may or may not involve exchanging particles through space."

"Teleportation?" I asked, bouncing on my toes.

"Possibly." Natasha's blue eyes twinkled. "We're still working on it."

"How is it that no one figures out you're here?" Renzo asked, shuffling behind the other shape-shifters. "A structure this size must require a lot of power. How do you stay off the grid?"

Natasha herded us into the atrium and aimed a chin toward several cushy chairs. Once we took our seats, her bodyguards circled her. "We use well water, and our ranch up the road is self-sufficient, producing enough power to support us."

"Don't the locals get suspicious when they see all the food you buy?" Autumn asked, cocking her head.

"The ranch has an immense greenhouse where we grow organic vegetables year-round. We also raise cattle for milk and other dairy, as well as poultry." The corners of Natasha's mouth slanted up. "When our truck arrives a couple times a week, the humans aren't privy to where the food goes. Anything else we need, we buy in bulk through different accounts and have the products shipped randomly from multiple sources to various locations."

"Brilliant." The shape-shifters had it all figured out so, I didn't bother asking any more questions.

"And we don't spend a lot of time making the place fancy," Natasha added. "Everything only needs to function. When we leave, we want as much to return to nature as possible."

Quentin offered her a proud grin. "I'm impressed with what you've built here."

I glanced over at Dathan who had frozen, his pinky looped through Autumn's. Her eyes widened, which meant someone was talking to him telepathically and she'd heard.

What the hell kind of news would pucker her eyebrows that way?

CHAPTER THREE
—— *Autumn* ——

"DATHAN, WHAT IS IT?" Natasha asked, worry lines etched across her forehead.

He ended his silent conversation with Cedric and cast a somber look at Natasha. "One of my men discovered a vampire less than an hour ago in Los Angeles, within a few blocks of the palace. She'd been dead several hours. Drained of blood." He pivoted to face my parents. "Looks like Ulric's work."

Renzo growled. "If she died around the time we left the palace, he might've seen us and followed us here. I bet that was him in the tunnel."

Just great. If that scumbag Ulric had recently refueled on vampire blood, he'd be even more powerful. We'd come to the shape-shifter compound to start a war but I'd had no idea the enemy would find us so quickly. My chest squeezed with trepidation.

Natasha dipped her chin in acknowledgment. "We should meet with my people as soon as you're ready. I'll show you to your quarters now." She rose and headed toward one of the stairwells. We followed her down the metal steps to the second floor, made a left, then strode through another corridor nearly identical to the other levels. White walls, plain wood floors—no bells or whistles. "As I said, we're already full so all six of you will be staying in my suite." She stopped in front of a door. "Open." The door swished open.

"It obeys voice commands?" I asked. "Nice."

"Yes, but the facial recognition software verifies before complying." Natasha hurried us through. "Close," she said as soon as we were inside, and then the door slid back together again. She brushed past us, jerking her head toward a door at the other end of the living room. "That's my private room, but I thought you might like to split up so you're not all crammed in one space. Olivia and Quentin can bunk with me."

Geez, the shape-shifter *queen* offering up her private sleeping area to my parents? My curiosity spiked. Maybe since my parents were no longer trying to keep their shape-shifterness from me, they'd be freer with information and I'd find out how they knew the queen.

I scanned the spacious living room where we'd be making camp—though there wasn't much to it. The living room offered almost double the space as our home in Los Angeles, except Natasha's suite had less furniture. An end table sat on each side of the couch with a coffee table in front it. Aside from four cots placed haphazardly in the corner, that was it. Not even a TV.

The left side of the room opened up to a small dining area furnished with a plain oak table and chairs, and beyond that a kitchen. To the right, a portion of a shower and sink peeked out from a bathroom. The only other door led to Natasha's room.

"We're sleeping on *cots*?" Dathan glared at the small beds occupying one side of the room.

"Unless you'd prefer the floor." Natasha's mouth twitched. "As for your belongings, I'm afraid you'll have to live out of your suitcases since we don't have extra bureaus. While you make yourselves at home, I'll program the computer to each of your voices and faces. Can't have any of you unable to access or getting trapped inside."

"Surely you have a more comfortable and private place for us to sleep," Dathan said, inching closer to Autumn. "Perhaps you can relocate some of your staff."

Natasha pursed her lips together. "You've had seventy-five years of comfy slumber. I'm confident that you're well rested. But if you can't live without your usual luxuries, your presence here isn't required."

I think I love her. Not that I wanted Dathan to suffer. He hated bullies and fought for equality for all species. He'd earned his place as king of all vampires and deserved any respect gained through his accomplishments. But he could be a pain—as he'd proved by ambushing Zack and me earlier when he introduced me as his fiancée—and I couldn't help but feel a small satisfaction that Natasha didn't let him get away with anything.

Zack snuck a peek at me. *She's growing on me too. If Dathan insists on having your cot next to his though, I'll be on your other side.*

I'm depending on it. In my peripheral vision, I noticed Natasha watching me. Okay, I'd have to be more careful when flirting with my real boyfriend.

Dathan huffed as he wandered off to explore the suite. We each claimed a cot, along with a spot in her living room for our belongings. I purposely grabbed one of the two cots in the middle to increase my chance of sleeping next to Zack. Which turned out to be unnecessary, because Renzo snagged the couch. My mom had disappeared into Natasha's bedroom with my dad but emerged when we'd finished settling in.

"They're all waiting for us downstairs," Natasha announced as she headed toward the door.

I wondered which part of downstairs we were meeting the rest of Natasha's people. We were on the second floor and the only thing I'd seen on the first level was the garage.

Natasha steered us down the stairwell and out the door, but instead of guiding us toward the cars or storage area, she sidestepped and headed to a wide green steel door. A chill snaked up my spine when I remembered that somewhere in the tunnel—maybe even closer—someone was waiting to pounce.

But he was just one person. How much damage could one intruder do against Natasha and her people?

As soon as Natasha opened the green door, the sweet scent of grass and jasmine hit me. She stepped over the threshold.

"We're going outside?" I asked. That didn't seem safe at all.

Natasha paused, her head tilted into the doorway and back in our line of vision again. "Sort of."

She marched on and as I took a step to follow her, Dathan's palm touched my lower back. *You should ask your parents how they know Natasha. I think you may find their answer quite intriguing.*

The fact that you want me to ask only makes me not want to, I lied, shrugging him off. I took all the steps in one leap, quickly catching up to my mom. Though I was bursting with curiosity over any secrets my parents might have, I refused to give Dathan the satisfaction. And how annoying that somehow he had intel on my family that I didn't have.

"Our own private park," Natasha said with a flourish of her wrist, indicating an area that was probably the size of an entire block.

I glanced up and noted the soft clouds floating in the sky. Except they didn't move at all. A cluster of trees in the distance marked the edge. Animals dotted the outskirts—a handful of wolves, a couple of tigers, a bear and several birds—along with a smattering of other shifters in their human form. They slowly drifted our way.

Natasha led us to a raised section against the wall and we all stepped up onto a platform. When I spun around, maybe forty more people had gathered. They'd obviously been nearby all along, but hadn't been easily noticeable in their animal forms.

I stuck near my parents when they sidled up to Natasha. Much to my relief, Dathan stood on her other side, giving me a break from the pretense of being with him. My dad's gaze bounced between Dathan and Zack then he gave me a strange look. Must've been awkward for my dad to know I had a boyfriend while another guy pretended to be my fiancé.

Are you finding Dathan as irritating right now as I am? Zack asked me.

No, I answered. *More so.* I peered over to see him smiling.

"My friends." Natasha focused on the mass of shape-shifters and smattering of werewolves. "Some of us have been waiting a very long time for the opportunity to take a stand against prejudice, bias and slavery; to rise up against werewolves and free ourselves. I believe if you listen to what our guests have to say, you will conclude as I have that now is that time." She took a step back and waved a hand for Dathan to proceed.

He moved forward, pulled back his shoulders and folded his arms over his chest. "I am Dathan Lacroix, king of the vampires." Murmurs rang through the crowd and he plowed on. "Many of you have valid reasons to hate vampires as much as the werewolves who have been oppressing your kind for centuries. I'm not here to change your mind about my kind. I want only one thing from you." Dathan cast a glance around the park and met the gaze of every single shape-shifter in the park. "Help me kill Ulric Vasilyev."

"Why would you need so many of us to get rid of one werewolf?" a woman shouted over the grumbling of the crowd.

One corner of Dathan's mouth lifted. "Because he's not your average werewolf. And as soon as he's gone, I'll return the favor and help you win your freedom from King Mortimer."

"But as the vampire king, you can gather your people and win any war without outside help," another woman said.

"I could do that." Dathan nodded. "But I choose my battles carefully and I'm not sure my people would be on board with a full-on war against werewolves, considering we are particularly susceptible to their bite. I'm sure you can imagine their desire to let things be."

A muscular man pushed forward until he was at the front of the others. "How can we be sure you're worth investing our trust? We could help you kill Ulric but we have no guarantee we won't be killed trying to get rid of King Mortimer."

Dathan's eyes trained on the shape-shifter. "Most of you probably grew up on tales of me. How many of those stories ended with me failing or not fulfilling a promise? None." Dathan faced me, his fingertips reaching out and beckoning me closer.

I inwardly groaned and walked toward him.

"It so happens..." He flashed me a charming grin. "I've grown quite fond of a particular shifter. I'll do everything in my power to protect her and her species."

I stared at Dathan and my breath caught as his plan hit me. This wasn't just about his acceptance from my kind. He needed an army, which he probably had little chance of getting without using me. How the hell was I going to publicly break up with him now?

Renzo stepped up and Dathan moved aside. "For those of you who don't know me, I'm Renzo Soriano," he said, addressing the man who'd spoken up before moving on. A low hum of murmurs rang through the mob. "In scanning your faces, I recognize some of you whom I've personally helped escape werewolves, through my work as leader of SWAAST. If you aren't sure about Dathan, perhaps you'll put your faith in me."

Natasha stepped forward again. "Either we band together now or continue the next centuries being slaves or criminals, hunted forever." She paused a beat. "We've been waiting for someone to change things, but I think we know that *someone* is all of us. This is *our* time."

The rumble of voices increased but I couldn't tell if they were going for the idea or skeptical.

"What have we accomplished these past decades or centuries other than merely survive? We have superior technology, certainly, but we don't have freedom. Months or years from now, this haven will be discovered and then we flee. Again." She took a deep breath, then exhaled. "Am I the only one who's tired of living in fear?"

"No!" The people shouted.

Natasha held up her palms and the roar died down. "I appreciate your enthusiasm, but I feel the need to remind you that we're talking about taking down an empire. It won't be easy and some of us may not survive."

A hush fell over the room and my dad touched Natasha's shoulder before speaking up. "I'm Quentin, an old friend of Her Majesty. We have the help of a handful of werewolves and a vampire. It's not much. Hell, maybe none of us will walk away. But we will have tried and maybe we'll even win. I believe our dream of equality and freedom is worth fighting for. I think we have a strong chance."

Dathan stepped forward again. "Unfortunately, none of us can afford to wait for a better time. The more time that passes, the more powerful Ulric gets. We're doing this. Now. You can be part of taking back your freedom or you can turn away and risk possibly centuries passing before having this kind of opportunity again."

"No one will be forced to stand and fight with us." Natasha grimaced, then wiggled a clipboard in the air, then handed it to Sean. "For anyone who'd rather run and take their chances, write down your name and we'll arrange for your departure as soon as it's safe."

"Whoever is staying must prepare for war," Dathan said.

A deafening roar filled the park and the ground trembled beneath my feet. When the yelling and stomping died down, Sean was surrounded by several who were trying to sign the paper. My gaze landed on each of their faces and my stomach churned. A little part of me died with the knowledge that they'd decided to abandon ship and now we had less to fight beside us.

Natasha cleared her throat and the remaining people quieted. "As you can see, our army is slightly smaller now. I still believe we can do this. As we prepare for battle, I'll need each and every one of you to work harder, train harder. Questions?"

"Yes, what's the plan?" a woman asked, raising her hand. "Do we even know where Ulric is?"

"Possibly." Natasha paused and the room became quiet. "The tunnel has been breached but we don't know by exactly whom. We strongly suspect Ulric."

"Which is why no one can leave yet," Dathan added, the side of his mouth lifting into a smirk. "In fact, those desiring to withdraw from the fight may not have a choice."

"We'll get with each of you individually regarding your part in this." Natasha hesitated a moment to see if anyone had questions. "That is all. " She reached down into a nearby cooler and tossed a water bottle at each of us. In my peripheral, shape-shifters disbanded, many of them leaving the park.

Natasha slung an arm around my shoulders. "We were already doubled up which is why some of them were sleeping in the theater. But I might have a way to get a private room for you and Dathan. Can't make any promises though."

"That won't be necessary," I said, raising my voice and enunciating carefully so my words carried to Dathan. "We vowed to wait until marriage before... you know." That should teach him to ambush me. Two could play at that game.

Zack sputtered and set down his bottle of water. *Good one.*

Natasha's arm dropped from my shoulder as she coughed. "Right." She pressed her lips together but since her brows were drawn, I couldn't tell if she was trying not to laugh.

That was classy, my future queen. Dathan's nostrils flared before he turned away and I couldn't see his face. *While you're so chummy with Natasha, why don't you ask her how old she is?*

My dad stood next to my mom, his blue eyes rounder than usual. *Was that really necessary?*

I was about to slink away when my mom's silent words stopped me.

Sweetheart, nice way to impress the shape-shifter queen. My mom shook her head. *As leaders of this rebellion, and because of our close association to the queen, we must maintain some level of decorum.*

In my effort to send Dathan a zinger, I'd forgotten we were on a mission and coming across as mature was a definite plus point. And I'd embarrassed my parents. "Yeah, I'm pretty awesome," I mumbled.

Doesn't it make you wonder why Natasha wasn't originally introduced as your queen? Dathan asked me. Though I had a feeling he was about to say something extra irritating, I was grateful for the distraction. *You and your parents must be pretty special that they're not encouraged to call her Your Majesty. Admit it. You're dying to find out why.*

Before glancing around to make sure no one around sensed my hostility, I blew out air and glared at him. *No, that's just you're dying for me to know. And when you get tired of waiting, maybe you'll spit it out. Until then, I'll happily live in ignorant bliss.* I sent him a smile dripping in syrup.

Dathan stared at me, tapping his foot. Good. I hoped my resistance was as maddening to him as his prodding was to me.

Zack's fingers twisted around mine and I repositioned our joined hands behind us where no one could see. *The shape-shifters aren't paying attention to us,* he said, his eyes sparking with mischief. *Let's sneak away for a couple minutes. Who knows when we'll get another chance to be alone.*

As I scanned the area for a place to take Zack, my mom shot me a disapproving look. *If you two get caught doing anything inappropriate, we lose credibility,* she said.

Since Zack had been touching me, he must have heard that, because he recoiled and stepped away. *We'll figure something out,* he said.

If the security in the place was worth bragging about, Natasha had to have cameras all over. I glanced toward the walls that were painted deceptively like a forest, making the park appear endless. Above the door was a small black button that looked like glass.

Dad, you think that's a camera above the doorframe? After meeting his gaze, my eyes flicked to the spot.

His gaze followed mine. *Most likely.*

If I didn't want to get caught making out with Zack, I'd have to watch for those little black buttons.

Natasha ushered us back up the stairs. I spotted cameras in the stairwell and over the door as we landed on the third floor. We turned a corner and passed a bathroom. No cameras in front of it that I could see.

"This is the training room." Natasha opened the door and everyone shadowed her inside.

I hung back, scanning the hallway for cameras. A black button stared at me over the doorway. The training area—which was a large enclosed space near the atrium— was slightly bigger than Natasha's suite with plenty of room for at least several pairs to spar.

"We've been training for decades, some of us for centuries. We would be happy to impart our knowledge to you." Natasha located Sean at the entrance and summoned him over. "Everything calm with the crew?"

"Yes, Your Majesty." Sean gave her a slight bob of his head as he stepped onto the mat, then handed a sheet of paper to Natasha. "These are the new assignments I worked out."

I glanced at my mom who'd been awfully quiet. She stood on the outskirts, staying close to my dad. I'd noticed her getting near Natasha, but she still avoided

Renzo and Zack like she might catch fleas from them or something. Even as my mom talked to Natasha, she stood as far away from Sean as she could.

Your mother isn't just avoiding the werewolves, is she? If you asked her why, I'm convinced you'd be riveted by her answer. Dathan smirked when I snuck a glance at him.

Why couldn't Dathan be upfront and say what was on his mind? And couldn't he pick a time for this crap when we weren't preparing for battle? As I repositioned myself to focus on the others, which took Dathan out of my line of vision, I vowed to dig until I found out what my parents obviously didn't want to tell me—without Dathan knowing I was doing exactly what he wanted.

"Zack." Natasha glanced up after a moment of perusing the list Sean had handed her. "I understand you're good with cars, so you're on auto maintenance. Our vehicles are kept in good working order. You shouldn't have to deal with anything more than the basics, but everything should be checked regularly anyway. We can't risk the food trucks breaking down and exposing us to any werewolves who might be nearby." Natasha grunted. "Not that any of us will be going in or out of the compound anytime soon."

"Great." He glanced at me, his eyes smoldering. *I miss you already.*

Miss you too. And very likely I'd be missing him even more the longer we pretended we weren't together.

"You'll have some other duties as well. Renzo," Natasha said, spinning to face him. "I'd appreciate your input on strategy and we'll need any intelligence you have on werewolves and such that might help us prepare for Ulric."

Renzo hung a thumb in his jeans belt loop. "Of course."

"And you'll all be on training." She regarded each one of us a moment. "You too, Dathan. You've been around a while, I know, and you're extremely powerful. But while you were getting soft these past seventy-five years in slumber, we were perfecting our combat skills."

Dathan's eyes sparkled. "I'll happily check out your moves, Your Majesty."

An involuntary spasm made her shiver. She had to really dislike him. But my bigger concern was my "fiancé" flirting with another woman right in front of me. I could understand him forgetting about me, especially talking to someone as beautiful as Natasha—except the scam was *his* idea. Now that he'd made this blunder though, ending things with him later would be easier. But not yet. I slammed my palms against his back and followed it up with, "Nice, babe."

Dathan sighed while Zack snickered.

Natasha rubbed my arm. "No man is worth losing your sanity over. It's why I'm still single."

Dathan's lip curled up. "Or you're alone because you haven't met anyone who's man enough to handle you."

"And I *still* haven't." Natasha's eyes flared with a warning. "Let's train while we wait on Ivan and Valerie to prepare our meal."

I groaned at Dathan's immaturity. "I'm hitting the restroom." I spun and exited the training room. Halfway down the hall, inspiration struck me and I sprinted the rest of the way, pushed on the door and waited a beat as I checked the bathroom for black buttons. *Zack, meet me in the bathroom. The one we just passed on our way to the training room. There aren't any cameras around.*

Sure, we could get caught as we left the restroom, but since I had no idea when we'd get another opportunity like this, I was willing to risk it.

Zack swept in and scanned the walls and ceiling, rotating in the small space. *I guess they decided not to be creepy by putting a camera in the bathroom.* He cupped my face with both hands and stared into my eyes. *Are you okay?*

I wasn't going to waste my precious few seconds of privacy with Zack by replying. My gaze riveted to his lips before fusing to them. My lungs compressed when Zack locked his arms around me so tightly that I completely flattened against him. I didn't know how long I could hold my breath because I'd never timed it. But it was longer than these few minutes I might have with Zack. So I didn't bother trying for oxygen. I just concentrated on those full lips, his tongue sliding against mine, the musky scent of his skin, the denseness of his muscles.

He held me, his kisses gentle but passionate, as his hands explored my body like it belonged to him. He pushed forward and I bumped against a surface. Even as he squashed me against the wall, his hands managed to squeeze between the wall and me, moving lower until they brushed my butt. I moaned, my fingertips parting tiny paths through his silky dark hair.

Autumn, where the hell are you? My dad's voice boomed into my head.

I shoved Zack away and he stumbled. *My dad's looking for me. Wait a few seconds after I leave before you come out.* I planted a brief kiss on Zack's lips before rushing out the door.

I was in the bathroom, I told my dad as I darted through the door to the training room.

He met my gaze from the other side of the crowded room. *And you needed Zack's help?*

I blushed. In a flash, my dad was standing in front of me, his jaw set and his hands fisted. *Autumn, this is not the time for that. We've got a job to do and a psycho on the loose. If anything happened to you... if Ulric captured you... I don't know how your mother or I would go on.*

Now I felt like an ass for stressing out my dad. I hung my head and my dad visibly relaxed as Zack returned. "I'm sorry. It won't happen again."

"You don't go anywhere alone, not until Ulric is captured or dead. Got it?"

I groaned. "Yes."

† † †

Natasha had chefs who prepared the meals so everyone else could work without getting caught up in food preparation. While we trained, a delicious aroma wafted in, which compelled me to sneak peeks into the kitchen nearby. Ivan, a tall shape-shifter with reddish hair and a ruddy complexion, occasionally grumbled over missing ingredients or incorrect temperature while he micromanaged his petite Latina assistant, Valerie. She waved him off with a light scolding, happily sampling the next dish.

My mouth watered while I continued to train. Finally, they set plates at an oversized picnic table with matching benches. The shape-shifters may have had the barest of utensils but they went all-out with the food—appetizers, salads, several vegetable dishes and two meat choices. I didn't know if all shape-shifters made such elaborate meals or if we got special treatment because we were dining with the queen. Whatever. I planned to thoroughly enjoy their hospitality, regardless of the reason.

When they announced dinner was ready, I attempted to claim the spot next to Zack. Dathan snaked it before I got a chance to sit, forcing me to his other side.

Sorry, Zack growled into my head. *I should've anticipated that.*

We should be more discreet anyway. That's probably the way things would go for the duration of our stay. Unless I ended the fake engagement with

Dathan. Unfortunately, instinct told me breaking up with him just yet was a bad idea. At least until his plan unfolded, whatever that plan was.

CHAPTER FOUR
—— Zack ——

TWO DAYS HAD flown by in a frenzy of work and training, with rarely a moment for breathers. And almost no time for Autumn. I missed being alone with her. I missed exchanging flirty looks or witty comments, and the feel of her silky hair between my fingers. I especially missed snuggling with her.

Natasha and her men hadn't found the source of the heat they'd spotted by infrared, because the cameras in the tunnel were still down. No other signs of life had been documented outside the compound either.

We were beginning to think the extra heat had been a technical glitch, which would explain why all the cameras in the tunnel went out. Natasha and Renzo tried to review the footage but it had disappeared. The security guy's story of a virus sounded plausible and Natasha trusted her people. But something didn't sit right with me and I couldn't figure out exactly what. I couldn't imagine her people putting their own lives at risk by covering up the presence of a dangerous werewolf. Maybe my paranoid imagination was working overtime.

Still, what if the nagging at my subconscious, that thing tickling my brain and making the back of my neck tingle, was real? Though I stayed on alert and was thankful Quentin kept a close eye on Autumn, I tried not to think about Ulric or that he might still be in the tunnel waiting for his chance to get to us. Correction: I couldn't help but think about the danger we'd walked into by coming here instead of running for our lives. So I did my best to keep myself busy so I wouldn't dwell on everything that could go wrong.

Each day began before dawn, Autumn and I tended to our cleaning station, sweeping and mopping the floors. Though I wasn't crazy about that task, at least Autumn and I got to do it together. We were never alone—not to mention the cameras everywhere—and couldn't touch each other, but it was our one chance to have a real conversation until bedtime. Which we did silently.

After our morning chores, we went straight to breakfast, then we trained until lunch. Meals were my favorite parts of the day. Ivan and Valerie were masters in the kitchen and everything they served was the best food I'd eaten in my life.

While we rested after lunch before the next pummeling, we'd each complete other duties—me in the garage while Autumn washed dishes—then we returned to the training area after our bodies had sufficient time to heal.

Her parents had stayed in Natasha's room, while the rest of us slept in the living room. Part of me wondered though if Olivia wanted to avoid everyone else in the building the way she avoided my dad and me. Ultimately, I didn't care. Less people in our sleeping area meant less intrusion on my time with Autumn, even though we had little privacy.

In case Natasha came in while we were sleeping, I didn't scoot my cot closer to Autumn and hang onto her hand until we fell asleep. I resigned myself to a brief touch before settling down a few feet from her. At least we hadn't needed to separate as we'd always thought we would. I couldn't let anything or anyone tear us apart again—not even some crazed werewolf amped up on vampire blood. But as I vowed not to let Dathan get too close to her, I knew I'd already lost. They had some kind of bond and it bothered me. What were the chances of Autumn falling for him? I didn't know. But any chance at all was too much.

During combat training, Natasha usually paired with Dathan since he was the most powerful. With her fighting skills, not only did she hold her own against him, she usually bested him. He didn't seem to mind. And I quietly gloated over the fact that Dathan apparently wasn't "man enough" for her either.

Renzo sparred with Sean, and Haji had been assigned to me. While it was a huge relief that my dad wasn't constantly beating the snot out of me the way he had at the vampire palace, dread deluged me each time I tried to strike Haji, a massive black guy with arms the size of my thighs. His bulk didn't slow him down at all and I may as well have been a gnat annoying him.

This training was important though, so I gave it my all. By the end of the night, I didn't have the energy to sneak a kiss with Autumn.

Olivia had been paired with Persius, a guy who looked like a bronze statue—too tanned to be living in a mountain with so little sunshine. And Quentin had been matched with Rakin, a tall lean Arab who always held his head high, as if he'd once been royalty. Autumn teamed with Egon, the werewolf.

After only two days inside the shape-shifter haven, cabin fever gnawed at me. Sure, I morphed at night in their underground park, but I needed a little change in our routine. And I burned for some time with Autumn. Alone.

We had two hours to go before dinnertime and sweat streamed down my arms, dripping off my fingertips. I popped off the floor after Haji tossed me across the room like an old shirt.

Yvonne marched in with her shoulders back, her mouth set in a grim line. "Your Majesty."

Everyone stopped, anxious to hear any news on Ulric. "Yes, Yvonne?" Natasha let the sword hang at her side.

Yvonne nibbled on her bottom lip a moment before releasing it again and running a palm over her nearly bare scalp. "Lenny and Blake spotted a group of werewolves in Mammoth."

"And they lived to tell?" Dathan shook his head. "This isn't good."

Natasha hooked him with a death glare. "Care to tell me why two of my men being alive is bad news?"

"If Ulric left Lenny and Blake alive, it's because he intends to use them for something." Dathan rocked back on his heels, raising his chin. "It means the worst is yet to come."

"Or it means they simply succeeded in avoiding Ulric. I've been around a while and I'm proof it's possible to survive and beat the werewolves." Her mouth widened. "And vampires."

Dathan raised a challenging brow. "You're sure all your people are trustworthy? Confident they won't divulge our whereabouts, even under the most grueling torture or the most tempting bribe?"

Natasha angled her head to the side. "My people can't be bribed with riches or promised freedom, because they know these things will never be given to them by the enemy. They are loyal under the most extreme circumstances, because they must be."

A vein pulsed at Dathan's temple. "We have a few in our midst who wanted to abandon ship at the first sign of trouble. That's not loyalty."

"Lack of desire to engage in war doesn't automatically mean deficiency in moral fiber." Natasha scowled, taking a challenging step toward Dathan.

Most of the time, she talked like anyone else, but I occasionally detected a faint accent. Definitely not American. British? And for a shape-shifter, weak as they were, to be capable of holding her own against Dathan, she had to be ancient. Granted, she had some serious skills but she had to be crazy strong too.

"You're making excuses for your men." Dathan stretched taller and his lips distorted. "The brave stay and fight. The only conclusion must be that whoever chooses to leave is a coward."

Natasha huffed and waved the sword she'd been using. "Vampires have been murdered for months and where are your people to stand up for their dead? It appears all *your* people are cowards."

"My people have been under attack for mere months, as you said. Yours have been oppressed and needlessly butchered for centuries and all they can do is run?" Dathan scoffed. "The fact remains that Ulric was last seen near Los Angeles just days ago and if he isn't already here, he will be soon. If you want all your men to die, do continue to coddle them. If you want to win this, we must consider every angle so we don't get caught off guard."

Natasha's mouth slowly curved up, her gaze boring into him as she aimed the tip of the sword at him. "If you don't approve of how I rule my people, you don't have to stay."

"You two, settle down." Olivia shot a scolding look at Natasha then Dathan. "This is not helping. We all need to work together."

"Rather difficult to accomplish when Her Majesty is in denial." Dathan flipped around, leaving Natasha glaring at his back.

Her eyes flared. "I think you should leave."

I prepared myself for a verbal explosion—and I hoped it wouldn't be worse than that. The last thing

I wanted was Dathan bailing on us. He acted like a douche bag many of his awake hours, but our chance of winning against Ulric was better with him. I needed to get Natasha and Dathan fighting less with each other, and focused on the real war.

"Since Ulric is probably very close by, maybe even in the tunnel, and we already know it's not safe to exit the building, I'm curious how much food we have on hand." I nervously shifted my weight to my other leg, hating the idea of being trapped inside much longer, especially if we ran out of fresh food. I enjoyed real food too much to eat emergency rations that probably tasted like my shoe.

Taking my cue, Autumn chimed in. "Assuming we can't leave to replenish our supplies, how much longer can we stay here?"

"We have a few more days of fresh food." Natasha lifted her chin. "When that runs out, we can use our emergency rations."

"How long will the backup supply feed this many people?" Dathan asked, spinning and facing her again. "Because I've got another week or so of blood and then I'm out."

"Thankfully you can eat human food," Natasha said, syrup dripping off every syllable.

Dathan rolled his eyes, throwing his hands up in the air. "Damn it, woman. Must you argue about everything?"

"Only if I'm talking to you." Natasha swiveled and stomped away from him, stopping beside Autumn's dad. I lowered my head to muffle a laugh.

"I thought you guys were old friends," Quentin asked, glancing between Natasha and Dathan.

"'Friends' is a bit of a stretch. But I'm always gracious until someone gives me a reason not to be." Natasha threw Dathan a searing glance. "He saved my life years ago. Maybe he thinks that gives him license to tell me how to do my job."

I don't even want to imagine how those two could tear up the place if they got physical, I told Autumn. *We need them both alive and well, so they can help us fight Ulric.*

I'll try to distract them again. "Can we stay on track?" Autumn asked Dathan and Natasha. "If we're going to be trapped here for a while, we need to work out the food situation."

"We've got enough rations in storage to feed fifty people for six months," Sean answered, then he grimaced. "The dried food tastes like dehydrated rubber. I don't recommend it unless we have no other choice."

"I was thinking," Autumn began, making sure she had everyone's attention. "Why are we letting anyone dictate when we can and can't leave when we could solve this by inspecting the tunnel?" Autumn chewed her bottom lip. "Maybe we'll discover it really was an animal. In that case, we'll all be free to come and go. Food and blood won't be a problem."

"That requires sending my people into a place where Ulric could very well be. And possibly getting them killed." Natasha lips mashed into a straight line.

"Then we'll all do it. Ulric will be grossly outnumbered," I said.

"And if he gets inside the building somehow, because we opened the hatch?" Natasha shook her head. "No."

"We'll take precautions, guard all entry points," Renzo said. "We can do this. Worst case scenario we find Ulric and kill him."

Dathan hissed. "Whether or not Ulric is in that tunnel, he's very close. But we need to know either way. Natasha, gather your people and use them to guard the door to the parking area. The rest of us will search the tunnel. Let's get it done."

A sharp intake of air drew everyone's attention to Natasha.

"What is it?" Quentin asked. He reached a hand toward her hair, then withdrew.

Natasha's chin quivered. "I've just been informed that one of my crew has been found dead in the parking area." She bolted out the door and Dathan followed.

I didn't need to ask if the person was murdered. Any immortal knew that none of us died of natural causes.

CHAPTER FIVE
—— *Autumn* ——

WHILE DATHAN AND Natasha finished at the crime scene, the rest of us returned to training. My mom paced the outer edge of the room where she easily avoided being hit by Zack or me sparring with our dads. Although Renzo routinely kicked the snot out of Zack, staying ahead was growing more and more difficult for Renzo. I wondered at the effect of the vampire blood we'd consumed and how long it would last.

Spotting Natasha and Dathan slipping through the door, my dad halted his assault on me. "What did you find out?" my dad asked.

"Decapitated. Havers and Kieran are still scouring the garage for evidence." Natasha ambled to the weapon wall, picked up a knife then hung it back up. Her eyes were vacant, like she was a million miles away.

Dathan leaned a shoulder against the wall, keeping Natasha in view. "Lulu looked a little thin, maybe a couple pints low on blood."

"The killer is a vampire?" Renzo snarled.

"Possibly." A vein pulsed at Dathan's neck, his eyes stormy. "Or someone who's been consuming vampire blood so long that he's taken on our characteristics—like our need for blood."

"What did the cameras show?" Renzo asked.

"A guy about six feet tall in a hoodie and jeans. He slithered in from the park and into the garage." Natasha scoffed. "He must've known the exact location of every camera because none of the footage showed his face."

Dathan raised a brow at Natasha. "Which means he already knew the layout. Either his source—most likely one of your trusted people—relayed the information with incredible accuracy or the killer has been here himself. Both scenarios impossible, according to you."

Natasha spun to glare at Dathan, her teeth grinding. "Either way, you get to gloat."

"I'm hardly gloating, sugar. I'm just glad we can finally get down to business and take this seriously." He leveled a look at Zack, then me. "This psycho is somewhere close by and I don't want him anywhere near you two. No one goes anywhere alone."

"That rule applies to your entire crew, I hope," my dad told Natasha.

"Yes, absolutely." Worry lines etched the skin around Natasha's eyes. "I've got a group checking the rest of the compound, excluding the tunnel. They have orders to alert me at once if they find anything suspicious."

"Wait." I waved a hand. "He came out of the park. Why didn't your security team flag him going in?"

"Probably because he didn't do anything to appear suspicious," Dathan said. "He's obviously been coached."

"No one detected additional scents around the body?" my mom asked.

Natasha's mouth turned down, her eyes glistening. "Lulu's been dead for a couple days. Long enough for the killer's scent to dissipate."

"How can you not notice a crew member missing for two whole days?" my mom asked.

Natasha slumped and lowered onto the matt. "Lulu kept to herself. She's in charge of supplies so she tends to be gone for long periods of time doing inventory."

"Who discovered the body?" Renzo asked.

"Kieran was doing a routine security check of the grounds." Natasha sighed. "Lulu was wedged between a car and a wall all the way in a corner."

"If the intruder came out of the park and into the garage, he likely hasn't gained access inside the compound," my dad said hopefully.

Natasha rubbed her temples, her lids dropping a moment. "We'll know soon enough."

"Maybe not. The murderer could be anywhere by now. Until we find him or he decides to show himself, we need to hone our skills." Dathan zoomed to the weapon wall, chose a sword, then tossed it to Natasha. She caught it and rose from the mat. Everyone else in the room paired with their partners and began sparring.

With Ulric already here, makes you want answers to all those unasked questions, doesn't it? Dathan asked me silently as he turned to Natasha and raised his sword. He traded a few thrusts and jabs with Natasha. *You should also ask your parents about their relationship with Natasha, and how old she is. While you're on the subject, you can ask your parents how old they are. Things might fall into place for you.*

Dathan, please stop. All those mysteries were already driving me crazy. But I needed to work out a good approach on my parents. I couldn't have Dathan coercing me into doing anything stupid and hurting my chances of getting them to cooperate.

I'd hinted plenty of times over the past couple days but neither of my parents had given up a damn thing. Instead, they took every opportunity to answer a question with another question or reply so vaguely that I was too disgusted to continue probing.

I've stopped prodding you about your parents for two days and you've accomplished nothing. He dodged Natasha's sword, ducking and rolling then sliced his blade through the air, narrowly missing Natasha. *Next time you hug your mom, why don't you get a nice long whiff?*

My stomach flipped. *What?* Why in the hell did I need to smell my shape-shifter mother who I'd known my entire life? Maybe Dathan was developing cabin fever too. Or there was something else he wanted... *What's in it for you?*

He held up an index finger at Natasha and she paused before the next blow. Then he swept toward me with such speed, I backed up. He reached out and tucked a lock of hair behind my ear. All mischief gone, he met my gaze. *Your safety.*

Dathan stood a little too close for my comfort. Though his words and proximity hinted that he felt more for me than a casual acquaintance, I didn't get any kind of sexy vibe from him. At all. What the hell was his deal?

Zack wedged himself between us. With his back to me, I couldn't read his expression but the energy vibrating off his body told me he was having words with Dathan. Since Zack was touching me, I should've been able to eavesdrop. I couldn't hear, which meant they were shutting me out.

Dathan stepped away, his palms up. "Natasha, I'd like to take a few moments with the young ones. Sort out some personal issues."

Natasha scowled. "Not just the three of you."

"We'll go straight to your suite and check in as soon as we get there. Then we'll let you know when we're on our way back. They'll be safe with me." Dathan motioned me toward the door. *Let's get you two some alone time.*

I didn't know what Zack had said to him but was too thrilled about any privacy with Zack to worry about Dathan's motives. I could've hugged them both but I waved to my mom and dad instead, then burst into the hallway after Dathan.

You two have five minutes, then we need to get back to work. As soon as we entered the suite, Dathan disappeared into Natasha's room.

He knows how pissed I am and he's trying to make up for being such an asswipe, Zack said as soon as Dathan disappeared.

We can discuss his motives later. My lips found Zack's mouth and my tongue slid against his. A blaze ignited in my belly.

"Missed you," he told me when we came up for air. His fingertips feathered across my cheek for a moment, then he hooked his other hand around the back of my head and drew me closer until I was nuzzling his neck.

We only have a few minutes and you want to cuddle instead of making out? I asked.

His chest quaked in amusement. *I'll follow your lead on that, Autumn, but it doesn't matter what we do. I just want to be with you.*

My heart expanded, filled with Zack, and swelled a little more. I hung unto his neck, swung my legs up and wrapped them around his hips, resting my cheek on his temple. *Dathan's being okay at the moment, but that won't last.*

He leaned back just a hair, and our noses touched. *We don't have to let him come between us.*

"True." I sighed against him. "When this is all over and King Mortimer is dethroned, my parents won't have to run anymore. Maybe they'll stay in California and settle down." But would Zack want to stay? "I've always wanted a dog, but pets were always too hard to travel with."

His lips brushed my cheek. "We can get two dogs. And cats too, if you want them."

We. That may have been the most beautiful word I'd ever heard from Zack. Tears pricked the back of my eyes.

"Sorry, kids. Time's up." The door to Natasha's room slammed and Dathan headed for the exit.

I didn't move, my legs still gripping Zack's hips. "Dathan?"

"Yes?" he asked, his hand on the doorknob.

"I don't know why you're such an ass so often, but I'm truly grateful for the rare times you're not." I grinned.

He threw his head back and roared, his laugh rough and rusty from lack of use. "Excellent."

Ignoring Dathan and his obvious desire to leave, Zack gave me a scorching kiss that sent tingles all the way to my toes. He flicked a few strands of hair off my forehead. *While you're playing Dathan's devoted fiancée, don't forget about us.*

"Never." I planted a kiss on his chin and jumped off.

"Leaving again isn't a good idea, so that'll have to last you a while." Dathan opened the door.

"And leaving this time was okay because...," Zack asked.

Dathan covered the distance to the stairwell at a vigorous pace. "Small window of opportunity. Ulric knows we're on high alert after discovering Lulu headless. And judging by his past, he's probably sitting back right now and enjoying the chaos as we scramble. I imagine it won't be too much longer before Ulric kills again though."

I felt a twinge in my stomach. "You don't know for sure it was Ulric. Maybe the killer is one of the shape-shifters," I said, panic raising my voice an octave. A week of combat training with the vampires and two days with the shape-shifters wasn't enough to combat one of the most powerful—and most evil—werewolves in the world.

"Shape-shifters don't drain their victim of blood. It's Ulric, I'm sure of it. And he's amped up on vampire blood. He's going more insane each day and would do just about anything." Dathan held the door open for Zack and me. "If he made it inside, won't be long before others gain entry."

I swallowed the lump forming in my throat as I went ahead of Dathan. "That's comforting."

Dathan chewed the inside of his mouth. "He enjoys the hunt. He'll draw it out as long as he can."

"But he couldn't be traveling with many men, right? A big group would raise too many flags. Even if Ulric had ten men waiting to attack, we've got almost fifty here." Zack scoffed.

Dathan's head swung side to side. "Not smart to underestimate him."

We returned to the training area and all eyes darted to us. "You guys worked everything out?" my dad asked, casting a suspicious glance at Dathan.

"All good, Dad." But I dreaded the next long chunk of time keeping a distance from Zack, pretending he and I were just friends. I conjured up a smile for my dad then glanced at my mom and her trainer, Persius. I needed to worry less about any potential boyfriend problems; concentrate more on our mission and what Dathan had been hinting at me to find out. If there was something to smell on my mom, why didn't Persius pick up on it? "How old are you?" I asked him.

Persius blinked, probably wondering why the random question. "Twenty-two. Why?"

"Just curious how my mom is doing against you." Persius had to be too young to easily pick up on an odd scent. "She's not giving you any trouble, is she?"

"Absolutely." Persius flashed his white teeth. "But what I lack in strength, I make up for in skill."

My mom's eyes narrowed at me. "Someone's in a better mood."

Normally she'd roll with my moods, especially if I seemed happier. Which meant she was probably suspicious of my line of questioning. I couldn't worry about that though.

I'd noticed her step away from Persius when they weren't actually training. As if she didn't want to take any chances. Well, if she wasn't going to spill it, I'd find out for myself.

I flung myself at her and, as discreetly as possible, sucked in a huge lungful of air while my nose was buried in her neck. "I love you, Mom."

"Okay." She gave a shaky laugh and patted my

back, clearly confused.

Dathan was right. She didn't smell like my dad or Natasha. But she didn't smell like Egon, Zack or Renzo either. Maybe she wasn't a shape-shifter or werewolf. Except that I'd seen her morph into a wolf every night since they'd arrived at the vampire palace. Then again, I'd only ever seen my dad as a wolf too.

I peered over at Natasha, her posture stiff as she snuck a peek at my mom, then my dad. Whatever was up with my parents, Natasha had to be in on it.

"Okay." Natasha slapped her palms together. "Back to work. Dathan, I'm sure you can amuse yourself somehow while I do rounds. Egon and I will be back in fifteen."

My dad shook his head with exaggerated movements. "Not just the two of you." He was awfully bossy for someone who hadn't seen Natasha in over eighteen years, especially considering he was addressing his queen.

"Yvonne, Sean and a couple others are already waiting for me in the corridor." She pivoted and marched toward the exit, but halted mid-step and glanced at me again. "Are you up for accompanying me?"

Of all the people here in the compound, why would she want me on her rounds? If she and my parents were as tight as I suspected, why wouldn't she ask one of them to go with her? Since I was already drowning in mysteries galore, I wasn't going to stress over this new one or question Natasha on her choices. I was going to seize the moment. "Sure."

She motioned me out of the training area and past the atrium toward the security room. Egon, Sean, Yvonne and another guy I'd seen when we'd first arrived kept a discreet distance from us while Natasha led the way. "Egon, you've been more quiet than usual. Something wrong?" She glanced back and so did I.

"Everything's fine, Your Majesty," Egon assured her, his eyes constantly searching the environment for anything unusual. "We all have a lot going on."

"Fair enough." She knocked on the door marked Security, then shoved it open. "Havers?"

When we entered the room, a short Asian man stood up and inclined his head. I remembered seeing him our first day at the compound.

"Your Majesty." He lowered his head.

As though he'd just become aware of his queen's presence, Kieran leaped up from his chair. "Forgive me, Your Majesty," he said, bowing.

"What's the status?" she asked in an all-business tone.

"No unusual activity," Havers replied. "Monitors are working and no entry points have been compromised."

"We're in contact with the ranch and everyone's checked in," Kieran added.

"Thank you," she said.

Once in the hallway, we rejoined the others and I followed her toward the office. Her shoulder brushed mine as we walked. *I'm worried about Egon. He's normally much more vibrant.*

I wouldn't know the difference, I said. But if I notice anything odd, I'll certainly tell you.

I'd appreciate that. She paused before the office door and pivoted to face me. "I'm glad you're all here. I trust Dathan with my life. Quite comforting to have him nearby at a time like this. I wouldn't want to take on Ulric without him. Renzo and your parents are a bonus."

I scrunched up my nose. "You trust Dathan to fight for you, but it's obvious you have an intense dislike for him. Doesn't add up."

She shook her head. "It's complicated."

I switched to telepathy so Egon wouldn't overhear. *Complicated... like when you care about someone against your will and you don't want him to know?* I winced when it occurred to me this probably wasn't the kind of conversation to have with someone who was technically my queen. *Sorry, that was inappropriate.*

She sighed, the lines between her brows disappearing. "It's fine." *Dathan and I go way back with some bad blood between us. We may not be enemies but we're not exactly friends either.*

I nodded like I was satisfied with her answer. But I was dying to know the details of their strange relationship. Had they fallen in love? Was she bitter at how it ended?

She slanted her head as though listening to someone inside her head. "Supper is ready, but we're due back anyway. We'll breeze through the rest of my rounds, then head to the cafeteria."

Since we were short on time, her guards and I waited outside the research room while Natasha poked her head inside. After she established no one was missing and everyone was doing their jobs, we headed downstairs. I shadowed her around the park and while she spoke to a few of the residents, I had a chance to see how the others sparred. These shape-shifters were so badass. I hoped we had more time to learn from them before the big battle with Ulric.

When we returned to the third floor, we went straight for the dining room. Valerie was setting tiny shakers of salt and pepper on the long table while Ivan placed plates. Our group was already seated and waiting for us.

My mom met my gaze and bobbed her head at the next chair over. Obediently, I sat in that spot and greeted my dad who'd claimed the chair on her other side. Dathan grabbed the spot next to me and Zack sat directly across from us beside Renzo. Natasha claimed the head of the table and our sparring partners took the other end.

Once all the plates had been piled high, Dathan waited until the others had taken their first bite before digging in. I ignored the scrumptious aroma of roast beef. As I forked an ample portion of zucchini, my knee relaxed ever so gently against my mom's leg.

What's the story with you and Dathan? If I had to guess, I'd say you and he have a past, my mom said. Immediately on alert, I snuck a peek at Natasha.

After a long hesitation, I could hear Natasha speak through my physical contact with my mom. *I'm not sure what you mean.*

Of course you do. We've known each other a long time. I can tell when you're holding back.

After another spell of silence, Natasha set her fork on the table and eyed my mom. *We met a long time ago and traveled together. Dathan's unpredictability has always worried me. He has no problem crossing lines that you and I would steer clear of.*

Despite him being a vampire, you trust him enough to allow him into your fortress and plan a government coup, my mom pointed out.

I see so much good in Dathan. He may seem unstable or unpredictable, but he always comes through when I need him.

And that's what's holding you back? my mom asked with a hint of sarcasm as she eyed the beef.

What exactly are you asking? Natasha delicately carved a slice from the hunk of beef and popped it in her mouth. *If you think I have feelings for Dathan, you're mistaken. The only feeling I have for him is trepidation. He's a wild card. And why are we discussing your future son-in-law in this way?*

My mom coughed and took a sip of water. Apparently, Dathan and I weren't the only ones who forgot to pretend we were engaged. *I sense tension and I'd like to help any way I can.*

Natasha stared at her plate, her fingers curled around her fork. *So much has happened since you and I last saw each other. I fell in love, got married and... had a child. They were both killed by werewolves and I decided I'd rather be lonely than ever go through that kind of pain and loss again.*

I swallowed, not wanting to imagine that kind of

grief. What would I do if I lost Zack?

A husband and a child. I'm so very sorry. My mom spared her a brief glance like she was trying to be discreet. As if the rest of us couldn't feel the energy between them. *And then came Dathan to help mend the wounds. How did you meet him?*

I was hunting the werewolves whom I believed had murdered my family. Fueled by rage and the need for revenge, I'd gone after them alone. I wasn't thinking straight. Natasha gave a nearly imperceptible shake of her head. *Dathan happened upon me while I was fighting three werewolves and barely hanging on. He risked a werewolf bite to save me. Once we'd disposed of the bodies, I thought he'd want some kind of payment but he walked away.*

I scrunched up my nose, grossly disappointed. That couldn't be the whole story.

And that's why you're angry with him, because he saved your life? My mom chuckled silently.

Natasha scowled. *Not even close. I spent the next year training, honing my skills so I'd never again have to worry about being overpowered by werewolves. Next time I encountered the dogs who murdered my family, I'd be ready. I was lonely and still grieving.* She squeezed her eyes shut. *I encountered Dathan again under friendlier circumstances. He was handsome, charming. I knew it would never lead anywhere but somehow I allowed myself to be swept off my feet.*

Sounds like you needed him, my mom said in a silent whisper.

I did and he filled the void for about a year. But as I said, I often found myself questioning his choices. Our concepts of right and wrong were, and still are, drastically different. So we agreed to part ways and reunite in the future when it was time to take down King Mortimer.

And here we are, my mom said. *But weren't you even sadder after he left?*

Actually, without him, I was free of all obligations. I was relieved to see him go, Natasha replied, plucking a biscuit from a silver tray. *I'd vowed never to allow myself to invest so much in anyone again.*

My mom paused, staring at her food a moment. *Yet you did.*

Natasha halted mid-bite and glanced at my mom. *Did what?*

You fell for Dathan anyway. When Natasha set down her fork, my mom forged on. *Please don't try to deny that you're drawn to him, minimally you feel more for him than you want to.*

Natasha's eyes sparked. *Believe whatever you wish. I'm not sure I can ever let anyone in again, least of all a man such as Dathan.*

"Are you two finished yet?" Dathan asked, irritation straining his voice.

As if the topic of Dathan was closed forever, Natasha shoved her plate away and turned toward the devil himself. "Definitely."

I didn't think so. Natasha wasn't done with Dathan, not by a long shot. And she still believed we were engaged. Maybe she actually wanted him despite her denials. Maybe she'd feel less resentment toward him if she knew he was attainable.

Yvonne cleared her throat as she approached the secluded dining area. "Your Majesty. I'm sorry to disturb your meal but I thought you'd want to know right away... two of our crew are missing."

Natasha canted her head, her brows drawn as he stared at Yvonne. "Not possible. I just finished a round and no one informed me."

"I didn't want to say anything until I knew for sure."

"Who?" Natasha asked.

Yvonne's left eye twitched as she scrunched up her cheeks in a grimace. "Claire and Ryan."

Natasha rubbed her temple. "The entire compound was searched, every nook and cranny?"

"Of course, Your Majesty. Even the parking structure and lockers, as well as the park and sleeping quarters."

Natasha flinched. "And you made sure no one could slip into the area you'd already searched?"

"Positive." Yvonne sighed. "We're stumped."

"Then we need to search again," Renzo said. "Unless you think they could've left without your security team knowing. Maybe they wanted to get away before the war started."

"You won't find them." Dathan stood, then tipped forward and flattened his palms on the table. "I know your people wouldn't want to help Ulric, but anyone who encounters him may not have a choice. If he were to telepathically persuade your men, he could find out anything he wants, whether his victim was willing to share or not."

"Although I seriously doubt Ulric's ability to telepathically persuade my men, I agree that we should prepare for all possibilities," Natasha said, her brows drawn in worry as she rested her elbows on the table.

"Which should include confirming someone did indeed breach the tunnel and if they got inside the compound," my dad said in his most authoritative tone. "And if the crew members really did leave, we need to figure out how they got out and why no one saw them on the monitors."

"I need to send a group into the tunnel, but that means allowing my people to go outside the safe zone." Natasha tapped her chin thoughtfully.

Dathan scoffed and returned to his chair. "That's assuming the safe zone hasn't already been compromised."

Natasha rubbed her temple. "I have to think on this."

"You must make sure they take proper precautions as they move through the compound. I'm sure you don't want to lose any more of them." Dathan peered at me from under his lashes and I knew he was about to annoy me. This time though, I was grateful for the distraction from the missing crew members.

He leaned into me. *How did your little experiment with your mom turn out? Was I right again?*

I rolled my eyes, not caring if anyone knew I was annoyed at my fiancé. *Unfortunately, yes. My mother doesn't smell like Natasha or my dad. But she doesn't smell the same as Zack and Renzo either.*

And you're her daughter. Dathan picked up a fork and steak knife then began carving a big hunk of rare beef. *How many times have you heard someone say you didn't smell like a shape-shifter?*

Too many times. And Dathan obviously knew why. *I'm not a shape-shifter?*

Dathan speared another hunk of meat. *That's not what I said. But you need you to find out why you're different.*

I didn't smell like a shape-shifter, but I *was* a shape-shifter? Yet I was different. Awesome. Now I couldn't concentrate on food. But I needed to eat for energy, so I loaded my fork with stuffed zucchini. *Not to sound repetitive, but what's in it for you?*

Dathan smiled smugly as he spooned mashed potatoes in his mouth. *A more accurate question is... what's in it for you?*

I gripped my fork as irritation ripped through me. *Dathan, seriously.*

We've been over this. Dathan paused his dinner to shoot me a glare. *I want Ulric and King Mortimer dead. You and Zack safe. Now all you have to do is ask the correct questions.*

I groaned. *Oh, just tell me already.*

It's not my place.

Thankfully, he stopped pressing and I could continue

my meal in peace and contemplate my differentness.

After swallowing his last bite, Dathan rose and pushed his chair back under the table. "Excuse me. I have some business to attend to," he said as Ivan came around to gather the empty plates.

What's going on with you two? Zack asked, pausing with his next bite of beef.

I'm trying to figure that out. I glanced away from him to find everyone at the table staring at me. "Don't look at *me*. Dathan started it. I'll go talk to him." *Dathan, wait up.* I bolted into the hallway and was about to follow Dathan's scent when he hissed.

"Damn it, Autumn. You're not supposed to be alone. Do you want to disappear like the others?"

Patience gone, I cut to the chase. *What gives, Dathan? You knew about Ulric, you have a lot of info on my parents and you know something about Natasha. For all I know, you could have other surprises in store for us.*

I've lived a long time, encountered a lot of people, and I pay attention. Nothing too mysterious.

I scoffed. *And?*

The corner of his mouth lifted. *And after you get your answers from your mom and then Natasha, I do have another surprise for you.*

I threw my head back. *You're killing me.*

Dathan chuckled. "Let's get you back to training, sugar."

I grunted, spun and marched ahead of him back to the training area. *I'm breaking up with you soon, FYI.*

He whistled. "Whatever you say, sugar."

I stopped short, twisted around and slapped a palm on his chest. *I know a nice shape-shifter queen I can set you up with. Word on the street is you guys used to have a thing.*

His smug smile flipped, morphing into a scowl. "What we had wasn't anything at all. Merely two people using each other." His tone softened with a hint of mischief. "You don't have to be jealous, sugar."

I flinched, then turned away and swung the door open.

He gripped the door by the top and held it open for me, his arm over my head so I could pass. "You're the one who brought it up. Might be best if you didn't involve yourself in my love life."

"I don't think you need to worry about that. Your past is far less exciting than I had hoped." I didn't look back as I headed straight for the training area.

My mom sparred with Persius across the room—away from everyone else, as usual. Not a surprise. My dad paired up with Rakin and by the time I circled to locate Egon, he was standing next to me. I needed to talk to my parents soon. Unfortunately, the inquisition would have to wait.

But that didn't mean I couldn't have a quick private conversation with Natasha. I held up an index finger at Egon, then went for it. *Um, Natasha? I think you should know that Dathan and I were never engaged. He wanted me to pretend so that the other shape-shifters would accept him more easily. I went along with it because it made sense at the time, but I already have a boyfriend. Zack.*

She froze in the middle of a stretch. *Why are you telling me this?*

I feel bad for not being honest. I faced Egon, my energy renewed and my spirits lifted. "I'm ready."

And I was curious to see what Natasha would do with that information. At the very least, the sparks between her and Dathan would make things a little more interesting.

CHAPTER SIX

—— *Zack* ——

AS SOON AS we walked into Natasha's living room, I wanted to fall onto my cot and pass out. But Dathan had already slipped into the bathroom and he always took the longest showers ever. Dathan... the most irritating person I knew. What the hell did he have going with Autumn to make her annoyed enough to chase after him?

I wanted to pound my fist into my chest, announce to everyone in the compound that Autumn was mine, then throw her over my shoulder and haul her off to a private room where I could do things to her that would make her toes tingle. Things that would make her cry out my name and tell me how much she loved me.

That was a fantasy for another day. I was too tired to get into a conversation that would likely turn into an argument. I just wanted to wind my body around hers and finally get a full night of sleep. Well, the cuddling part wouldn't happen tonight, but the sleep definitely would. I yawned. "Maybe I'll go straight to bed and hit the shower in the morning."

Autumn wrinkled her nose. "Before five a.m.?"

I blinked when she dragged the mattress off my cot. "What are you doing?"

"Earlier today I had a nice chat with Natasha. Ended up telling her that Dathan and I aren't actually engaged, that you're my real boyfriend." She beamed. "We don't have to hide anymore. Not in here anyway."

I could feel my face split, exposing my teeth. "That's the best news I've heard in ages."

"Isn't it?" She giggled.

My dad pointed to the sofa. "For the love of God, please don't forget I'll be sleeping over there."

She laughed. "We won't. I promise."

I helped Autumn move her own mattress onto the floor next to mine, then we scooted them together. When we finished making up our bed, Autumn pushed Dathan's cot all the way to the other side of the room. I heaved his suitcase up and hauled it across the floor, setting it beside his cot.

The scent of soap mingled with steam followed Dathan as he strolled out of the bathroom. He halted when he noticed the new arrangement. "What's going on?"

Autumn pointed to Natasha's door and lowered her voice. "I sort of slipped to your ex that Zack was my real boyfriend. We don't need to keep up any pretenses when we're in here."

"His ex?" My mouth went slack as I switched to Dathan. "You and the queen?" I whispered.

His nostrils flared. "If I hear any indecent noises from you two, I'll join you on that nice big bed."

I saluted him, then rifled through my suitcase for boxers and a T-shirt, brushed my lips against Autumn's and dashed into the bathroom before someone else beat me to it.

Ten minutes later, Autumn was dead-still on our mattress, her deep steady breathing telling me she was asleep. I chastised myself for my missed chance to get a good-night kiss from her. On the upside, we could snuggle all night. But first...

"So what's the story with you and Natasha?" I asked Dathan.

"I was wondering the same thing." Renzo sprawled out over the sheet he'd laid on the couch.

Dathan shrugged. "We ran together for a while."

Yeah, already knew that. "Did you love her?"

He huffed. "I never completely fall for any woman, Zack. I'm not made that way."

Renzo snorted. "I'm going to have to call you on that."

Exactly what I was thinking. And Dathan trying to deny having feelings for Natasha only made me more curious. "In all these centuries, you've never fallen in love with anyone? Not possible."

My dad snickered from the couch. "I'm with Zack. Highly improbable."

Dathan swung his legs up onto the cot and flopped against his pillow. "Some women have intrigued me more than others."

Maybe he wasn't forthcoming because Natasha was in the next room and could hear everything. *How long were you and Natasha together?*

He fumbled for his phone charger like he was trying to avoid my gaze. *A year maybe.*

How long ago?

I encountered her in 1812 and we met again about a year later, Dathan said.

So Natasha was well over two hundred years old. *She dumped you, huh?*

Enough questions, Zack. He threw me a hard look then followed it up with a pillow.

I caught the pillow after it bounced off my head. *If you want her back, Autumn would probably be willing to put in a good word for you.* I aimed the pillow at him.

Dathan snatched the pillow from the air and stuffed it behind his head. *Make sure Autumn keeps up pretenses outside this room. The others need to believe she's devoted to me.* He rolled over on his side and closed his eyes. Conversation over.

A moment later, I rested my head against my pillow. "Hey, what if Ulric attacks in the middle of the night? If he's here like we suspect, and he has any power over others, they're all in danger."

Renzo raised an arm from his horizontal position on the couch. "He strikes when he strikes, whether it's ten minutes from now or ten days. When he shows himself, there are a lot of people he must get through to reach us. Until then, we need to carry on."

I rose to pace, and stopped to face my dad as I tilted my head. "You sound pretty casual about how Ulric would 'get through' all those people. Doesn't it bother you that they'd all die for us?"

"They're on night shift, Zack," Dathan muttered. "They know what they signed up for."

Still, seemed harsh. "So they stay up on watch while we're here all comfy in our beds?"

Renzo propped himself up on an elbow. "And while we're up during the day, we're keeping them safe in their beds, probably getting better sleep than we are."

Yeah, okay. I could see that. I resumed my path across the wood floor. "Dathan, do you think Ulric made those two disappear or do you think they deserted ship?"

He lifted his head off the pillow and studied me for a moment, then exhaled as he stared at the ceiling. "Ulric is here and he's picking us off."

If only I hadn't asked. Now I felt even less safe than before.

"He has surprise on his side but we have numbers," my dad added. "Regardless, Natasha has measures in place, so if he's really here, we'll locate him soon enough."

Dathan readjusted his pillow to get me in his line of vision. "Unless Ulric is still in the tunnel. Someone here could be doing his dirty work."

I paused my assault on the floor. "How could that work? Because I've only been able to put ideas into people's heads, not extract information."

He grunted. "I'll explain this, then you need to go the hell to sleep."

I nodded and indicated for him to continue.

"Shape-shifters are similar to werewolves in that they telepathically plant thoughts into someone's mind. But only from a distance. Vampires must make physical contact through feeding, however, once we are connected we have far more control over the victim than a werewolf or shape-shifter ever could. You can influence them to some degree, but once we've given them a command, we can make them our slave for as long as we want, completely change their way of thinking or erase their memory."

"I'm not getting what this has to do with Ulric," my dad said.

"Wait for it." Dathan paused, checking to see if I was still paying attention. "If a werewolf ingests blood of a vampire, he may take on some of our characteristics. He may heal even faster, his strength will likely increase, but he won't necessarily crave blood."

There had to be more because I wasn't quite connecting the dots yet. I lowered to the mattress on the floor, careful not to wake Autumn. "And?"

"Imagine if an already deadly werewolf had been consuming regular doses of vampire blood for centuries. And what if he had gained the ability to completely control his victim as a vampire can, while maintaining his natural ability to influence remotely like any werewolf?"

My stomach churned and I fervently hoped Dathan's theory was wrong.

Renzo's head lifted off the couch. "You've seen this before?"

"Before I became king centuries ago, a werewolf terrorized my kind. Probably your kind too, I would imagine. I never had the pleasure of killing him because he vanished," Dathan said. "I believe he went into slumber as vampires are prone to do. I haven't met this werewolf they call Ulric, but he follows the same patterns as the werewolf I knew as Urian. They're the same person, I'm sure of it."

"Seriously?" I would've changed my name completely. "Doesn't seem like he's trying to hide from you with such a similar name."

"He wanted me to figure it out. A personal challenge," Dathan hissed. "And now you understand why I can't stop until he's dead."

"Yeah." I let my head drop back and sighed. "This just gets better and better."

"Enjoy your time with Autumn while you can. Until something else happens, no use worrying and ruining the good times." Renzo tugged the blanket up over his shoulder. "Try to sleep. If you can't, your body will still heal while you rest."

"Shut off the light." Dathan rolled over and turned his back to me.

When I scooted over to spoon with Autumn, she covered my hand and tucked it under her chin. Even the comfort of her warmth couldn't keep my mind from venturing into places too disturbing to allow me to sleep. Would we step into the hallway the next day and find everyone else in the compound had been slaughtered while we slept?

Leaving the suite each morning already made me uneasy because I never knew what was happening on the other side of the door. Natasha's security was better in her rooms than anywhere else in the building so getting inside was close to impossible. But we'd thought Ulric couldn't get out of the tunnel and with each day came more risk. I suspected my mornings of peace would be over too soon.

I hoped my dad was right about healing even if I wasn't asleep, because I was pretty sure I'd be awake most, if not all, through the night.

CHAPTER SEVEN

—— *Zack* ——

I'D FINALLY FALLEN asleep and woke with a start only a few hours later.

"Up." My dad flicked the back of my head with a towel.

Autumn mumbled into her pillow and I realized she'd barely moved all night. I wouldn't have an opportunity to get that close to her again until bedtime. I nuzzled my nose behind her ear and took a long slow whiff. She always smelled like vanilla.

Renzo nudged my foot with his boot. "Wake her and get to your chores. I don't want any of the shape-shifters feeling like we aren't doing our share."

"Has anyone checked in with the rest of them?" I asked, remembering our conversation about Ulric the night before.

"Everyone's fine." Renzo exchanged man-nods with Quentin when he and Olivia emerged from Natasha's room.

I rolled away from Autumn as the tension left my body. "I don't want to go into battle with Ulric. But at the same time, I can't wait until it's over."

"I concur. But as much as I want this done and Ulric dead, I want both of you to have every second possible to prepare. Up." My dad spun and headed toward the bathroom.

But no matter how long we trained, nothing could prepare us for what was to come. Battling Ulric would already be a challenge. Taking down an entire empire... I couldn't see a way for us all to survive it when we were so grossly outnumbered.

† † †

After we'd wrapped up lunch hours later, Natasha tapped her pen against the pad of paper she'd brought with her to the dining area. "Nothing on the monitors inside or out have picked up signs of coming or going by anyone, scanning all the way back to the video when you arrived. If that was an animal in the tunnel and it was somehow buried immediately—which would explain the heat source disappearing so quickly—we can also assume the structure hasn't been compromised and we could be safe here indefinitely."

Dathan eased back in his chair and brought a glass to his lips, his eyes squinting at Natasha. Watching him sip on red liquid—most likely human blood—didn't gross me out like it should have. The blood had an interesting texture which fascinated me in a weird way.

"You don't plan on leaving it at that, do you? At the risk of repeating myself, Ulric probably has one or more of your people under his control." Tension filled the room as Dathan's gaze fell on each one of us, spending an extra moment on me before returning to Natasha. "He wants Quentin and Olivia and you. If he's here, our best chance is to root him out before he can take us by surprise."

"Agreed. And we still have Lulu's death to take into account. Since I don't think the murder was committed by any of my people, we have an intruder somewhere." Natasha blew out a breath. "We need to do a more thorough inspection of the tunnel."

Quentin scoffed. "Quite a stretch to believe that he got out of the tunnel on his own, then hypnotized someone to help him."

"Or maybe it was the other way around," Dathan said. "From the tunnel, he made contact with someone and telepathically got that person under his control. Then his helper let him in. Or he's still in the tunnel and his assistant is doing his bidding."

"No one here would murder Lulu under *any* circumstances. No werewolf has that much control over another," Natasha mumbled, rubbing her forehead.

"You don't know that. It's even possible his helper has been glamoured into forgetting everything as soon as the deed is done. Your man may not even be aware of what he's doing." Dathan took another swig of blood. "We must be extra diligent and prepare for the possibility that *more* than one of your crew is working for him."

Natasha swallowed. "I trust your assessment in war. Just how sure are you of this?"

"I'd bet my life on it." Dathan tipped his glass toward her. "I'd also wager he's more dangerous than I'm giving him credit for. I believe that if your people are clever and move about the compound in groups, four or five of them are still no match for Ulric."

"Sean needs to do another head count," Natasha said, scrawling a note on the paper.

"I don't see the point since we can't do anything about other disappearances anyway. We need to search the tunnel, like you said," Quentin added. "Sooner rather than later, then check the entire compound again for intruders, make sure we're not somehow left wide open."

"Okay." Natasha dropped the pad of paper and began to rise. "Let's get started."

"Who says we're letting you go anywhere near the tunnel?" Quentin asked.

Was that concern over his queen or did he and Olivia have a prior relationship of some kind with her? Regardless, Quentin was right. Natasha was supposed to delegate while her people protected her.

Natasha's head swung side to side. "It's not your call to make. I'm the logical choice since I stand a stronger chance of surviving."

Quentin scoffed. "You'll survive because you're not going anywhere."

And now I was positive something connected those three. At least Autumn didn't volunteer. Of course, if she had tried, her parents would surely prevent her.

Natasha ground her teeth. "Who should I choose

to go in my stead? Which of my crew is less important than the other?"

"Agreed." Renzo scooted forward in his chair and slapped an elbow on the table. "No one here is more capable of fighting Ulric than us."

"I have a few things to do, then I need to make my rounds. Give me a couple hours," Natasha said. Quentin and Olivia both opened their mouths, probably to object, but Ivan returned and began clearing the table. Natasha swooshed out of the room.

"She shouldn't be off alone." Dathan tapped his glass on the table, drawing my attention to the contents, then slammed down the glass and disappeared. It sat half full, the blood swirling a moment longer and finally settling. Why wasn't the red goop repulsive to me? I hoped my sudden weird craving was due to just being hungry and not because I'd had enough vampire blood to become like Ulric.

CHAPTER EIGHT
——— *Autumn* ———

AS WE ALL prepared for our next training lesson, some of us stretching and others choosing weapons, my parents huddled with Natasha. They came off so genuine and easy, like being together that way was the most natural thing in the world.

"We're not discussing it again." My dad folded his arms over his chest. "You're not going."

Natasha snorted, which somehow didn't seem unladylike with her. "Telling me what to do, are you?"

My dad grinned. "I'm older and wiser than you."

Natasha huffed. "I could argue with the wiser part since you're not the leader of an entire species."

Did my dad just say he was older than Natasha? I'd thought he was joking, but the other two hadn't corrected him. I already knew Natasha was over two hundred so that meant my dad was even older. Did that mean my mom was around the same age?

That makes your dad almost as old as my dad. Maybe older.

I glanced at Zack. *Yeah, I caught that too.*

Imagine what you could get from your parents or Natasha if you actually asked, Dathan pushed into my mind.

God, Dathan was irritating. But I had more pressing things on my mind, and zeroed in on Dathan and Natasha. "Doesn't holding back put us on the defensive? We should already be searching the tunnel."

"Well, *offensive* is always better." Dathan's mouth lifted at the corners. When no one but me got it—either that or they didn't think it was funny—he rolled his eyes. "All joking aside, I don't want to rush us into battle, because every extra day we have is another day you and Zack have to train and get stronger."

True. But I'd had an overload of sitting around and doing nothing. First, when we knew my ex Daniel would be coming after us. And later when we'd thought we killed Charles, the werewolf assigned to watch over Zack, but he came back to stalk us. Then again recently at the vampire palace. "But every moment we wait, we could lose more of the crew. We need to be proactive, starting with getting in that tunnel."

"We?" Natasha lifted one brow. "You're not going anywhere."

"Exactly," my dad said. "I'll go."

Renzo and my mom both chimed in their willingness to accompany my dad. I didn't love that plan at all. I wanted both my parents where I could see they were safe.

"Give me a few minutes to think about this. You guys can continue training." Natasha began pacing the large room.

"Quentin, care to go for a run in the park with us before we resume bullying Her Majesty?" Renzo asked. "We should get the urges out of our system so we can be more focused in our search for Ulric."

My mom's face lit up. "Sounds great."

"You guys go ahead." Natasha rubbed her temples without making eye contact with anyone. Renzo left with my parents and Zack hurried after them a moment later.

Talk to Natasha while you have a chance, Dathan urged as he followed the others. "I'll make sure they make it to the park."

I glanced around to find Natasha's men hovering discreetly nearby, but they weren't intrusive enough to prevent me from getting her attention. With her obvious distraction, how would I approach the subject? And I would need a good segue to ask the harder questions.

Seconds slowly ticked by as I searched my brain for a way to get any kind of conversation rolling. I didn't have much time before my parents returned from the run and Natasha would go on rounds and we'd resume training. "So, what do you know about Ulric?"

Natasha blinked, as if I'd yanked her from deep thoughts. "In all my years, I've never known a werewolf like him." She wrapped her arms around herself. "I find it quite disturbing."

And there was my segue. "All your years... How many have you had? Three hundred, six hundred? Are you as old as Dathan?"

She rocked her head side-to-side, as if weighing how much information she should give me.

"It's public knowledge around the compound, isn't it?" I asked, hoping she'd see how ridiculous it would be to hold out when I could find out easily enough.

Her eyes darted around the room before switching to me. "I'm a few years shy of seven hundred."

"Wow." And my dad was even older? I stared at her, too stunned to think. During my silence, Natasha went back to contemplating the Ulric situation. When Dathan and my parents appeared moments later, I still hadn't closed my mouth.

Apparently too preoccupied to notice my reaction, Natasha spun to face them. "In delaying the search of the tunnel to keep my people safe, I've put them in more danger by not discovering the intruder's location."

"Great." Dathan swept toward the door. "Let's get going."

"Wait," Natasha said. Her gaze riveted on Dathan. "I want a promise from you."

Dathan groaned. "I can already tell I'm not going to like this."

"Sean is my second in command. If anything happens to me, I want you to guide him, make sure he learns to lead." She swallowed and took a deep breath. "You and I have our differences, but I know my people will be safe in your hands."

"Nothing will happen to you." Dathan's jaw clenched. "But if I'm wrong, I'll be too busy hunting down whoever harmed you to help your people."

Natasha inclined her chin and stared him down. "Promise me that helping my people will be your first priority."

Dathan glared a long moment, zeroing in on Natasha like they were the only people in the room. "Okay, I promise. Whatever. Let's move."

Sean tossed a flashlight to Zack and I, Renzo, both my parents, and Egon.

"You're staying here." My dad swiped at the flashlight I held, but missed when I dodged him.

I backed up, swinging the flashlight farther out of his reach. "Because anyone here can protect me better than you guys and Dathan?"

My dad's nostrils flared, his cheeks flushing. "Fine."

We followed Dathan and Natasha out of the training area and down to the parking structure where several more of her crew waited.

"We have no idea what's waiting for us on the other side, so be ready for anything." Natasha entered the code on the panel and the heavy metal door rolled up. "Egon and Sean, you're coming with me. The rest of you stay behind and make sure this area stays secure."

We all smelled the moist dirt and rotting flesh at the same time, various noises of disgust escaping us. I cringed, not looking forward to finding out the source of the dead smell. I really hoped it was an animal and not any of Natasha's crew.

"Go on." Natasha motioned us ahead, then swiveled around to the rest of the guards fanned out on the other side of the door. "Make sure this locks behind us. Whatever's in here isn't getting inside the compound."

"Wait." My dad said as one of the guards raised a hand toward the panel, then my dad turned to me. "You sure?"

"Oh, please." I rolled my eyes. "I've been in worse situations than this." Not that I wasn't scared. I was. But I'd probably be more afraid on the other side of the wall without Dathan, Zack, Renzo and my parents. Plus, I wouldn't know what was going on and I'd only worry.

Natasha nodded at the guard and the door rolled down. After checking to make sure it locked securely, we trudged forward. A beam of light extended from Natasha's flashlight, reaching up to the rock ceiling. "Camera is completely crushed." She marched ahead, stopping to spotlight another camera, also broken.

We instinctively moved together, some of us examining the ceiling while the rest scoured the tunnel sides. We didn't travel more than a few yards when Dathan halted abruptly, his flashlight trained on a wide hole in the tunnel wall.

"Wait. I thought this place was built with impenetrable titanium," Zack said.

"The compound, yes. The tunnel, no." Natasha aimed the flashlight down the hole, peering in. "Obviously, that was an error in judgment."

Dathan squeezed past her and poked his head inside, then felt around. "Let's find out how far this goes." He glanced over his shoulder. "Renzo and Quentin, how about a little detour with me?"

They both climbed through the hole after him. I doubted I was any safer staying behind with Natasha, my mom, Zack, Egon and Sean. Either path was dangerous, but exploring the hole wouldn't require standing around and doing nothing. I jumped in after my dad, moving quickly so that my mom or Zack would have to climb into the hole and pull me by my feet if they wanted me out.

Damn it, Autumn, Zack shouted into my head. *I can't follow you or I'll leave too few behind.*

Sorry, I'll be back soon.

We crawled through the narrow tunnel for several minutes. Finally, a shaft of light lit up the dirt, signaling we'd reached the end.

We know how he gets in and out of the tunnel. Now we just need to figure out how he gets in and out of the compound, Dathan told us silently. He reached the opening and poked his head out, then slowly scanned three-hundred sixty degrees. *No sign of anyone. Except a slight scent of werewolf. Whoever went through has been gone for at least a couple hours. Let's get out of here.*

I shifted gears and backed up. As soon as I found a space wide enough, I turned around. Unfortunately for Dathan, Renzo and my dad, they were too big and had to crawl the entire shaft feet first. As soon as I reached the end, I jumped out and into Zack's arms. He squeezed me hard for a long moment before releasing me.

Dathan was the last to exit the passageway. "Leads to outside. Two-hour-old werewolf scent at the end."

"Strange that his scent isn't inside here though. Not that I've detected yet." Natasha stepped forward, her flashlight constantly moving to scan the tunnel walls.

"The faster one moves, the less scent left behind." Dathan dusted himself off. "He must have moved very fast."

"That smell." My mom gagged. "I'd like to find what's been decomposing."

"The smell rules out the two who just went missing," Renzo said, moving toward the unexplored end of the tunnel. "They haven't been gone long enough to create that level of stink."

The rest of us crept forward. We breathed a collective sigh of relief when we spotted a pile of rats in various stages of decomposition. I coughed as the pungent scent violated my nose, relieved we were passing it.

"We're almost to the end." Natasha slowed, then stumbled. She stopped abruptly and tapped the soil with her toe. She spun, facing away. "I'm hoping this isn't what a think it is."

"A grave?" Dathan asked from several yards away. "Considering how strong the scent of blood is in this vicinity, there's a body nearby. And it's not an animal."

Of course Dathan would be quicker than the rest of us to pick up the smell of human blood. I could smell it now too, a rancid metallic stench.

"Why don't we head back, see you ladies safely inside, then return with a few more of your men?" Dathan motioned us away from the soft mound of dirt.

"Your statement is insulting on so many levels," Natasha growled. "If I'm too weak to look at a decaying corpse, I shouldn't be queen."

Dathan pivoted, then brushed her shoulder as he softened his voice. "If I thought you were weak, I wouldn't be here. You're the strongest woman I've ever known. But I think you've got enough to worry about without the visuals of what happened to someone you probably cared deeply for, as you do all your people."

Quentin slung an arm around her shoulders. "Besides, you have other things to attend to. For instance, while we're excavating, the rest of you can search the inside."

† † †

With over twenty people including my mom and Yvonne, we began the search on the third floor and worked down. As soon as we inspected a floor and made sure it was intruder free, we sealed all but one of the stairways, then left several guards there to watch the remaining stairwell. And then we hit the first floor. We cleared the entire parking structure, including the storage facilities and under the cars, then moved onto the park.

After the entire compound had been searched, the guards on the other floors were released and the stairwells opened. I waited with Natasha, my mom, Yvonne and a handful of others for Dathan and the rest to finish in the tunnel.

"They're coming back now." Natasha turned and palmed the panel. The metal door rolled up and my dad, Renzo, Zack and Dathan shuffled through the doorway bare-chested. I glanced at Natasha whose gaze was fixed on Dathan's chest. She blinked, shook her head and eyed the burden over Egon's shoulder which was wrapped in shirts.

"Please take the body directly to the research department. Any idea who it is, Sean?" Natasha asked.

"Facial features are no longer intact, but she's human, which means likely someone from town." Sean grimaced.

Natasha released a quiet groan. "We'll have to figure out a way to handle it with the locals. But we have more pressing issues at the moment."

Sean closed the door to the tunnel and then made sure it was locked. "I'll meet you shortly in the training room, Your Majesty."

Upstairs, my parents immediately hit the mat and began sparring. With the search over, my mind wandered with renewed curiosity over my parents. I'd have to wait a little longer for answers—hopefully I'd get them before the big war.

Hours later, Ivan rang the dinner bell and our trainers released us. Zack glanced over his shoulder as Dathan led him out. *You should talk to your mom, get more info. I think something is up with your parents and Natasha.*

Not Zack too. As if Dathan's nagging wasn't enough. *Will do.*

My mom passed me and I looped an arm through hers, slowing my pace. As though understanding that we wanted some mother-daughter time, my dad smiled and went ahead.

"It occurred to me I don't even know how old you are." I took a deep, calming breath to cover my jumping pulse.

"I'm not that old." She patted my arm.

As usual, my mom was stingy with details. I'd have to try another way. "Is Dad much older than you?"

"A few years." She tugged on my arm as we walked, like she wanted to get to the food faster to shut me up.

"A few as in... three to five years?" I asked.

"Yes. He's three years older," she answered.

I pulled her to a stop and turned to face her, my eyes narrowed. "Natasha is almost seven hundred and Dad is older than her, which makes you really really old, Mom. And the fact that I have to work so hard to get it out of you makes me wonder what else you're not telling me."

Her tiny intake of air gave her away. "Wow, where are you getting this information?"

"Not from you, that's for sure." I huffed. "I've been listening carefully while you all assumed I wasn't paying attention."

"So we've been around a while." She shrugged. "Big deal."

Hoping to keep her attention, I entwined my fingers with hers and caught her scent again. *You're not a shape-shifter.*

"What?"

She stepped away from me which told me I was right. But what the hell was she? *Your scent is different than Dad's and Natasha's. But it's not quite like Zack or Renzo's either. Too light.* I winced as the truth hit me. My scent was lighter than it should've been, as I'd been told repeatedly, because eating meat brought it out more. So I'd stayed a vegetarian as my parents had raised me. If she ate meat, her scent would be stronger and she'd smell similar to Zack and Renzo. *Oh, my God, Mom, you're a werewolf.*

A seven hundred year old werewolf... But my dad was a shape-shifter, of that I was sure. An old story tickled the edges of my brain, the legend of Hannah and Eli. Hannah was a raven-haired werewolf betrothed to the king but she'd fallen in love with a handsome blond shape-shifter and they'd escaped together. Everyone believed they were long since dead. But my parents fit their description perfectly and they were the right age. Why else would King Mortimer put Ulric, his most feared henchman, on my parents?

I lifted my chin, willing her to answer my next question. *What was your name seven hundred years ago, Mom?* When she hesitated and averted her gaze, I locked my fingers with hers before she could bolt. *Tell me.*

We'd drifted to the edge of the dining room area and I wondered if the others were staring. I didn't care. I wouldn't take my eyes off my mom. *No more lies, Mom. I need the truth. Please.*

Her breath hitched. *My name was... Hannah.*

Chills raced up my spine and goose bumps covered my arms. I took a long, slow breath and prepared myself for the answer to my next question. *Let me guess. Dad's birth name is Eli?*

She sandwiched my hand with hers, her eyes pooling with unshed tears. *You can't speak a word of this to Zack or Renzo. Or anyone else. If word somehow got out that we're still alive... Don't you see how much more danger you'd be in?*

I nodded numbly as the full scope of it hit me. Hell, Dathan could give us over to King Mortimer for brownie points to protect his own people and it would soothe tension between the species. Wait, no. He'd already known and had refused to tell me on the grounds that it wasn't his place to tell. But any of the werewolves here could sell us out.

Even if no one meant us harm, they only had to tell one person and the news could travel quickly. Or Ulric could glamour the information out. *You need me to keep this a secret because King Mortimer would do everything in his power to kill you. And me, of course, because I'm the product of mixing species, which is supposedly impossible.*

Exactly. Swear to me you won't discuss this with another soul, not even your father. If he learns our secret is out, he'll want the three of us to leave immediately. She swallowed, casting a glance at my dad who was already sitting at the dinner table and regarding us curiously. *We've been running from Mortimer so long, seems like forever. And I know this is the end; we can't run anymore. Not with Ulric crazier and more powerful than ever. But it could get worse if your father went after King Mortimer to protect us.*

I could see my dad sacrificing himself to save us. I'd do the same for them or Zack. In fact, I could totally envision Zack freaking out and doing anything to keep me safe. He might want to leave, but we were safer with Dathan, Renzo and Natasha to help us.

Everyone I knew and loved would be better off by my mother and me keeping this knowledge to ourselves. *I swear, Mom. I won't say anything to anyone, not even Zack.*

Her lids fluttered an instant before the worry lines around her eyes faded. "Let's get some dinner." *And never speak of this again.*

We sat at the two empty spaces at the table and I gave Dathan a dirty look. *I got it all. My parents are the infamous Hannah and Eli who have been running from King Mortimer for centuries. Are you happy now?* I dug into the pasta, shoveling an unattractive portion into my mouth.

Extremely. One side of his mouth arched up.

I promised her I wouldn't tell Zack. Please don't say anything to him, okay?

Not my place to divulge other people's secrets. I didn't tell you, did I?

No. So far, he'd kept his promises. But as I'd found out too many times, Dathan enjoyed ambushing people. *You stir up trouble though.*

Zack won't get so much as a hint from me.

Thank you.

As dinner progressed, I caught Natasha's gaze occasionally flash to my dad. She glanced at my mom less often but that was still more attention than she gave anyone else at the table. What the hell was up with Natasha and my parents? My gut told me that was the last piece of the puzzle.

Since my mom had sworn me to secrecy, she wouldn't mention our conversation to my dad. Which meant he wouldn't expect the questions I was about to throw at him. I could catch him off guard.

I aimed my silent words at Dathan. *As soon as dinner is over, maybe you can distract my mom while I corner my dad.*

He gave me a mischievous grin. *It would be my pleasure.*

Moments later, the last plate was taken away and my mom pushed from the table. Dathan closed the distance and stood between her and me. "I understand you're quite proficient at knife throwing. Perhaps you could give me some tips."

How Dathan knew anything about my mom, I had no clue. Not my concern at the moment. I tuned out her reply, jumped to the chair my mom had vacated and focused on my dad. *How long ago did you meet Natasha?*

Years ago, I lived in a village with other shifters. He scooted his chair back, probably an attempt to avoid more questions.

I clamped a hand onto his wrist before he could escape. *Did you used to date her?*

"What?" He grimaced. "God, no."

I stiffened. Natasha was beautiful and smart, so why would my dad be so horrified at the idea of dating a gorgeous blonde? *Are you two related or something?*

His mouth fell open while he stared at me. Probably trying to come up with a way out of answering the question.

The truth, Dad. Seriously, you know I'm going to find out eventually anyway.

He leaned forward, slammed his elbows on the table and dropped his forehead into his palms. *She's my sister.*

The wheels in my head turned, gradually picking up speed as I remembered the details of the story I'd read of Hannah and Eli. Eli had been free to roam the castle but he'd refused to leave, even though he could have flown away anytime he chose. But he didn't want to leave his sister Isabella who was being held prisoner by King Mortimer.

In the end, they'd both escaped with Hannah's help. All three of them had been on the run from the king for centuries. If anyone found out Isabella was still alive, they could follow the trail to my parents.

But to me, she was *Aunt* Isabella. No wonder she always seemed so curious about me, and why she'd taken me on her rounds—I was her niece.

I have an aunt! I threw my arms around my dad and squeezed. *I promise I won't tell a soul.* Which was the truth since Dathan obviously already knew.

He hugged me tight and kissed the top of my head. *Love you, sweetheart.*

"Love you too." I rested my head on his shoulder for another moment as I truly absorbed the enormity of what I now knew of my family. I had an aunt. She and my parents were ancients... and infamous. They were also the most hunted shape-shifters and werewolf in the world. And I was a freakin' hybrid. That certainly explained why I didn't fit the normal shape-shifter profile. And why I was so strong—I had werewolf strength on my side.

And now I could do more than kiss and make out with Zack. A hell of a lot more. But not yet. If I made a move on him, he'd object because he wouldn't want us to get weaker. I wouldn't be able to explain to him the mixing species thing was all a lie. A lie created by King Mortimer after my mom and dad escaped, probably so that his kind would never again stoop to mixing species with a "lower life-form."

My poor parents, on the run all these centuries. Wait... I thought female werewolves couldn't give birth. Their urge to morph was too strong and, supposedly, each time they morphed the baby was killed. If that was the case, my mom couldn't have birthed me.

Before I'd graduated high school, I'd wondered if my parents were human and had adopted me. But I'd found out otherwise, that they were my real parents. And here I was again wondering if I'd been wrong and maybe one or both of my parents weren't biologically related to me.

I reached an arm around my dad's waist and hugged him hard. He released me and I rose from the table to scan for my mom. I located her chatting with Natasha. *Mom, I thought female werewolves couldn't reproduce? Was I adopted or something?*

"Oh, hey, sweetheart." She slung an arm around my shoulder then faced Natasha again. "I'll be right back." She steered me to the far end of the training area.

Was I adopted? I asked as soon as she came to a stop.

No, honey. She hesitated a moment as though searching for the words. *You obviously already know that female werewolves are unable to carry to term.*

You didn't carry me to term yet I wasn't adopted? I'm confused.

She brushed a lock of hair off my forehead and a faint smile touched her lips. *These past centuries, I conceived over and over. It just about wrecked me each time I discovered I was pregnant while being fully aware that the child would die as soon as I morphed. Again and again.*

"That must have been horrible."

She laughed once. "You have no idea."

So... how did you get me?

We'd figured out a couple centuries ago that the urge to morph decreased as I ate less meat. After a couple decades as a vegetarian, I found I could go days without morphing. That turned into weeks. Eventually I was able to do it for months at a time.

And how many babies did she miscarry in those two centuries? I couldn't think about the grief she'd endured each time she'd morphed because she hadn't been able to hold her human shape one second longer.

Or the guilt she'd suffered knowing she'd killed her own child. I couldn't think about how many siblings I'd lost.

My heart ached for all of them and a surge of sadness hit me with so much force, I swayed into her. I clutched the sleeve of her shirt and I buried my nose in her hair. *I'm so sorry you had to go through that over and over.*

Her chin trembled against my ear. *But all that pain and grief got me you. I wouldn't trade that for the world.*

"Love you, Mom." I held her another moment before shifting my attention to Yvonne as she arrived in the training area, her mouth set firm. Whatever she had to say, it couldn't be good news.

"What is it, Yvonne?" Natasha asked, abandoning her conversation with Renzo.

"I've just received pictures of a group of werewolves who were spotted in Carson City moments ago." Yvonne zeroed in on her cell screen. "The images are still loading but since I've never seen Ulric, I wouldn't know whether one of them was him or not."

"If that's Ulric we're about to see, the person who sent the picture is probably already captured. More likely dead." Dathan rocked back on his heels.

"Where is Carson from here?" I asked.

Natasha stroked my hair, then seemed to realize what she was doing and inched away. "About fifteen miles."

If the image we were about to see was Ulric, then that really had been him in the tunnel and not some random intruder. My stomach pinched.

"It's finished loading." Yvonne thrust out her phone and the six of us crowded around her to get a look at the guy who could possibly be the most infamous werewolf in history.

"That's not Ulric," Dathan said in an irritated tone. "Do you have more pictures?"

Yvonne stayed on the first image a moment before swiping to the next. A couple seconds later, she swiped the screen again so we could view the next image.

"Wait." Dathan bent over my shoulder to examine the picture more closely.

The image was grainy which made sense since no shifter would want to get close enough to a werewolf to be detected. He was standing in front of a coffee shop, wearing a brown hat over his ash blond hair that partially obscured his forehead and shadowed his eyes. Judging by his long full beard he hadn't shaved in years. He was also dirty—like he'd been living in a tunnel for a few days.

"That's Ulric, AKA Urian." Dathan's jaw clenched. "No doubt."

CHAPTER NINE
──── Zack ────

"THANK YOU, YVONNE." Natasha hesitated a second or two. "Please have Kieran and Havers ensure all security cameras are working and we have no blind spots around the perimeters."

"Yes, Your Majesty." Yvonne retreated and exited the training room.

"If he's in Carson City, isn't he only about fifteen minutes away?" I automatically glanced at Autumn. "Which probably doesn't matter since that was probably him in the tunnel and he's been coming and going all this time."

"Exactly." Natasha flicked a wrist in dismissal. "He still has to breach the compound though. Which isn't going to happen."

"Ulric is Urian, the same werewolf I hunted centuries ago," Dathan hissed, getting up in Natasha's face until they were almost nose to nose. "And if he has developed vampire's ability to control minds, he doesn't have to get inside to inflict damage. Lulu's death is proof of that."

"Okay. Let's bring this down a notch." Quentin slid an arm between Natasha and Dathan, then squeezed in. Dathan backed up. "No new reports of casualties?"

Natasha shook her head. "No."

Dathan eyes shrunk to slits. "Ulric may have already been inside. Your missing crew members, Claire and Ryan, probably didn't escape. My guess is they were taken. Ulric could've easily tortured information out of them and has already figured out how to destroy us all."

My heart tripped then gained speed.

"Enough standing around," Dathan bellowed. "If Ulric is that close, we don't have time to talk. Let's get to work."

We trained later than usual, breathing occasional sighs of relief that none of us had come across Ulric. Close to midnight, we all staggered up to our room. By the time we got into bed, my limbs may as well have been boneless and I should've been asleep within minutes. I snuggled up to Autumn but instead of fading out, I lay there wide awake and staring at the wall. Ulric could come for us at any time. For all we knew, it could be another week before he attacked, but every minute until then would be torture.

† † †

As we slogged through our morning chores, I wondered why we were bothering with anything other than preparing for war. If we all died, we wouldn't need clean floors. The extra time could be spent training.

When Autumn and I arrived for breakfast, Dathan was already seated at the table buttering a biscuit.

"Hey, what happened to your blood diet?" I asked, taking a seat next to him. "Haven't seen you drink much blood lately."

"Blood heals and keeps us strong, but we can eat regular food. It doesn't do much for me though." He paused a moment. "Except make my taste buds dance. Bacon and eggs have always been a favorite."

Renzo chewed a piece of toast and swallowed. "My understanding is that vampires generally don't eat human food because it weighs them down, makes them weaker. Now probably isn't the time to lose strength, is it? Not when Ulric could attack at any moment."

Dathan chuckled. "You must have me confused with a newborn. But if it makes you feel better, I asked Ivan to bring me a glass of blood for dessert." And as if reading Dathan's mind, Ivan set a tall glass in front of him.

My mouth watered at the sight of the red liquid and I flinched. What the—? Why the hell was blood looking so good to me?

He studied me. "Want the rest?"

Yep, absolutely. Though I had no idea why. Human blood should have been thoroughly nauseating to me. Yet my attention riveted to the glass and I twitched with the urge to gulp it down. I scowled to cover up the disgust at myself. "No. Why the hell would I want to drink human blood? I'm not a vampire."

Dathan's eyes sparkled. "You've had enough vampire blood at just the right times to make things interesting."

My mom went through the procedure to become a vampire, not me. But judging by Dathan's mischievous smile, I was missing something. Sure, I'd consumed vampire blood, but so had Autumn and she didn't seem interested at all in the blood.

Without taking his eyes off me, Dathan picked up a strip of bacon and bit into it. *Haven't you ever wondered why your mother survived so many years past the time her doctors gave her?*

Of course I had. But how would Dathan know about that? And why couldn't I stop thinking of that glass of blood sitting within snatching distance?

I swiveled to see my dad. "Mom said that Magnus turned her?" He nodded and I continued. "How long have you known Magnus? I'm wondering why he couldn't change her until the very last minute."

Renzo discarded the last piece of his roll and let the fork clank to the plate. "I couldn't get permission to change her until then."

"But why did it take so long to get permission?" Autumn asked. "I thought you and Cedric were good friends."

Renzo lifted a shoulder and then let if fall. "If I were a vampire and under his rule, getting his blessing would've been easy. But I'm a werewolf, a longtime enemy of his people. Granted, we have a long history of exchanging favors over the last century, even before I met your mother—mostly me needing his help for someone on behalf of SWAAST. Cedric had already long since reached his limit when he gave me the vampire blood to keep Favianne going."

Swallowing the last tasteless bite of my eggs—what I really wanted was that blood—I laid my fork on the plate and pushed it away. "So you had to wait until enough time had passed to ask for another favor?"

"Precisely," Dathan answered before Renzo had a chance. "Further, you mustn't just get the king's permission but also the human's willingness. Giving your mother a choice would require revealing our kind's secrets as well as yours. If she refused our help and decided to remain human, we couldn't allow her to live."

"That's brutal." Autumn said. "But she wasn't conscious at the hospital. How did you get her to agree to be changed?"

"We didn't," Renzo answered. "Cedric gave me his blessing and we did it anyway. And I prayed she'd say yes after the fact and Magnus wouldn't have to destroy her."

"But," Dathan continued and I wondered why he was explaining it instead of my dad. "Cedric allowed Renzo to give your mother microscopic amounts of vampire blood in secret. Enough to keep her from dying—with the cooperation of a nurse in the hospital who slipped it into her IVs without being aware of what she was doing." He reclined in his chair, gauging my reaction. "Even when Favianne was pregnant."

"So…" I blinked, wondering why Dathan was repeating facts already known. I could feel myself falling into his trap—there had to be one. "What's your point?"

"I'm glad you asked." Dathan grinned. "When a human is given vampire blood, it has a temporary side effect of making the human healthier and stronger. You can't change a human that way, because that's not how it's done."

Right, a human had to be nearly drained first, then fed enough vampire blood so that the body could absorb it, transforming it into the new species. "But I'm a werewolf. Would the vampire blood have affected me differently as a baby?"

"When given to a young werewolf, same thing happens as with Ulric and his group—you develop temporary vampire traits. But given in utero, while the cells are multiplying and dividing, while the fetus is still taking form, you get…" Dathan scanned the faces of the room, his eyes taking on a mischievous glint when finally landing on me. "A hybrid."

My glass toppled and juice splashed over the table. "What? You're saying I'm a hybrid? Part vampire?"

Dathan's eyeteeth descended. "Beautiful, isn't it?"

"What the hell, Dathan?" Renzo shot up from his chair. "He's not a vampire."

Dathan's mouth crinkled at the corners. "I didn't say he was a vampire."

"Hold on. Relax, everyone." I sliced my hands through the air, in an effort to cut the tension. Dathan liked to stir up trouble, but he didn't lie. And I wanted the truth. "If I was a hybrid, wouldn't we already know?"

"If you were looking for it and paying attention, maybe." Dathan snickered. "Renzo, you're married to a vampire. Isn't it fitting that your child be both vampire and werewolf?"

Silence invaded the room. Renzo stared at me, his lips parted.

I scoffed. "C'mon, Dathan. Seriously?"

"I've seen you eat steak. The bloodier, the better?" Dathan shrugged. "Why don't you take a nip off Autumn? You might enjoy it."

"Zack doesn't have vampire fangs," she said. "His fangs don't show until he's morphed into a wolf."

"Because he hasn't tried." Dathan's eyes twinkled with amusement. "Go ahead, Zack. Work those special muscles in your gums. Those fangs will come out, I promise."

I had wanted the truth but was now regretting it. I tensed in my chair, ready to bolt when Dathan appeared at my side and gripped my shoulder. "Blood, Zack. That's all you need. The vampire in you has been dormant for years, but now it's time to wake it up."

I glared at Dathan, then vaulted from my chair, causing it to spring up and land several feet away. As I stormed out, I heard Autumn say, "I'll follow him and make sure he's okay."

Since the rest of them were still in the dining area, I headed to the bedrooms where I was sure to be alone. As I took the flight of stairs in one leap, footfall sounded behind me. I twisted around to see who it was and Autumn flew into my arms.

I released her, gently nudging her away. *Let's get inside the suite. I'm assuming Natasha wouldn't want her security people monitoring her and doesn't allow cameras there.*

Once we'd gained access to our room, I ushered Autumn inside and locked the door behind me. I had questions for Dathan but he hadn't followed and I wanted Autumn part of the conversation. I reached for her hand. "Dathan, why do you believe I'm a hybrid?" I asked both silently and aloud.

Not believe. Know.

"How do you *know*?" My jaw tightened. "And now is not the time for semantics."

Remember when I gave you my blood so you'd heal faster? Then, of course, I required the cure for werewolf bite. When I drank from you, well, let's just say I can tell the difference between werewolf blood and vampire blood. Your blood tastes like both. So before we left the vampire palace, I asked a lot of questions.

I dragged in a deep, controlled breath. "Is this a good thing or bad?"

Depends if being as strong as Ulric would be desirable to you. We should spend our remaining time before battle seeing how strong your vampire half is.

Both Renzo and his niece Alura had told me I was stronger than the average newbie. I hadn't paid any attention at the time because I'd been more concerned with why Autumn didn't fit the shape-shifter profile.

Since she was freakishly strong—although I still had no idea why, I was betting Dathan did—I hadn't noticed my own strength.

"Do you think it's true?" Autumn asked.

I slumped against the wall. "Dathan hasn't been wrong yet, has he?"

"That's not good news," she mumbled. "Okay, well, show me those fangs."

Irritation consumed me. "Don't you think if I could work my fangs, I would've already discovered them by now?"

She rolled her eyes. "No, not if you didn't know you could. Remember how long it took me to morph? I didn't try until I understood I was supposed to."

Letting my tongue wander along the surface of my teeth, I tried to move some imaginary muscle. It felt imaginary anyway.

"Those muscles are dormant, probably atrophied." She tilted her head to the side and flipped her hair away, exposing the vein in her neck. "Maybe if you think about biting me."

I snickered. "Autumn, I think about biting you all the time."

"Mm." Her eyes smoldered as her mouth curved up. "I like it when you talk dirty to me."

I laughed. "As much as I appreciate you lightening things up, you're distracting me. I don't have a lot of time to work this out. We need to get back to practice."

"Maybe we need stronger inspiration." Autumn tapped her lip a moment before spinning around and heading for Natasha's small kitchen. "Maybe some of Dathan's blood supply will tempt you," she called out and a moment later, she returned with a bag.

I already knew she was right—I wanted that blood. But seeing Dathan drink it in the cafeteria hadn't brought out my fangs.

That was before I became aware of them.

After figuring out how to open the bag, she waved it under my nose. It smelled amazing. Cravings stirred, similar to my hunger for meat but more intense. I'd consumed vampire blood at the palace, and I longed for blood now, but could I drink *human* blood? If someone had asked me a month ago, I may have been grossed out.

But now?

My gums tingled. I willed my muscles to relax, first my toes then my legs and I worked my way up. I imagined myself with fangs, letting them extend far beyond my gums, and an odd tugging sensation wrapped itself around my eyeteeth.

"Holy crap, Zack."

I rearranged my lips to cover my new-to-me teeth. Super weird against the inside of my mouth. My tongue immediately found what was different, sliding around the extended teeth.

"Damn. That is so hot." Autumn yanked me close and fastened her mouth over mine.

I retracted my fangs instantly, taking pains not to cut her up, then carefully set the blood bag on the table by the door so it wouldn't spill. Gripping her hips, I hefted her up and shoved her against the wall. She wound her legs around my hips, her fingers threading through my hair.

Someone coughed and it sounded like my dad. "Came up to make sure you were okay. But, apparently, you've adapted quickly."

I released Autumn and she tugged her T-shirt down. "Hi, Renzo," she said. "We were about to go back upstairs."

"Obviously," he said, dragging out the syllables. "Why don't we do that now? We have much to accomplish."

The smell of blood from the bag wafted up my nose and my fangs lengthened again. My mouth felt way too full and, naturally, my tongue sought out the new teeth. I tried to make my fangs go back into my gums, but they wouldn't budge.

Renzo tipped his head to the side. "That was interesting. I guess you learned how to work those things." He turned toward the door, then circled back. "I know you two aren't getting much time together and I hope that's remedied soon. Be thankful you're not an entire state apart from the one you love."

"Yeah. Hang on while I try to get these guys under control." I held my breath so I couldn't smell the blood and focused on Autumn since thinking of her had worked last time. My teeth slid up and I could finally release the air in my lungs.

My dad started toward the door again. I reached over and snagged the blood bag on our way out, drinking it as we took the stairs up. My fangs slipped out again, but by the time we hit the landing, I'd downed all the blood and got my teeth stowed away again.

When I returned to the training area, everyone froze as their gaze went straight to the crumpled blood bag in my fist. Haji squinted, like he wasn't sure what I'd do next. Natasha stared at me, her head tilted with curiosity.

Great. I was freak show now.

I cared less by the second as I became riveted to the glass of blood Dathan had just set on the table. My fangs extended again and I cursed, zooming across the floor until I reached the glass.

And then Dathan was next to me, his voice soft and soothing. "Relax, Zack." He took the glass from me and set it down on the floor where I couldn't see it. "Jesus, you're such a newbie. Can't have you attacking some unsuspecting human. Natasha, you're free since I'll be working with Zack the rest of the day."

"I'm sure I can find a way to amuse myself." Natasha switched to Haji. "With Zack occupied, we can train together since I'm partnerless now too."

Natasha probably didn't want me anywhere near him in case I got the urge to bite. She probably called it correctly and I shouldn't spar with anyone except Dathan.

Now I knew how my mom had felt and why she couldn't be let out among the humans until she had her urges under control. I glared at Dathan. "Your timing stinks. Now is not a good time to want to eat my sparring partner. We could be under attack at any moment and I might screw up, simply because my parts aren't working right. You couldn't wait, huh?"

"Actually, I wanted to put it off until we dealt with Ulric. But then I realized we'd need your special abilities for battle." Dathan glanced at his watch.

"You suck, Dathan," I muttered.

"Yes. And now, so do you." Dathan chuckled. "But I recommend holding out for human blood. No one in this place will taste very good."

Not only did I have to manage new abilities, but I'd also have to control the urge to eat my friends. This day was getting worse and worse.

CHAPTER TEN
———— *Autumn* ————

POOR ZACK. THINGS were probably going to be strange with him for a while.

As soon as we arrived back at the training area from our little excursion to our room to deal with his fangs, everyone's attention had riveted to us—except my parents who had vanished.

Probably for the best. I didn't want to deal with their feelings about Zack's new "condition" when I hadn't sorted out my own. I wondered if the mixing species law applied to us since he was half vampire. Or a third if you counted his human side. Still, he was part werewolf, so maybe it still did.

Whatever. It wasn't like Zack and I had time to venture into unexplored territory. We rarely had any alone time and when we did, it was for only minutes at a time. And if we didn't survive this battle, we'd never have a chance to mix species.

I shouldn't have been thinking about sleeping with Zack when he'd never told me he loved me. Yes, I could say it to him first, but what if he didn't say it back?

After being with Zack for months and all we'd been through, I knew he cared deeply. But real lasting love?

And now he had the vampire hybrid thing to deal with. He didn't need some girl falling all over him and being clingy.

Renzo slapped him on the back. "Well, son, maybe it'll work in our favor."

Dathan bent toward Zack and sniffed him. "The blood brought out the vampire in you, but be careful. Don't drink anymore, not a drop, or you'll leave this place smelling like me. I think sometime soon, you'll want to pass yourself off as a werewolf."

Zack "pretending" to be a werewolf was a new concept apparently none of us had considered. Silence enveloped the room for several moments until Natasha cleared her throat. "Autumn, your parents decided to go to the park and have a quick run. They'll return shortly." She studied Zack a beat before saying, "Interesting. I've never heard of a vampire-werewolf hybrid. I had no idea it was possible."

Yeah, shape-shifters and werewolves weren't supposed to be able to mix species, yet I was a product of mixing. Is that why Zack and I were inexplicably drawn to each other, because we were both freaks?

If we stayed together long enough to have children, they'd be what? Half werewolf and the rest human and vampire? Would their bite be venomous to other vampires? Could other werewolf bites harm them? Could I even have children with someone who was part vampire?

"You're overthinking it, aren't you?" Dathan asked, his shoulder bumping mine.

"Probably." I grunted. "All I know is that Zack and I need to train harder."

"Let's roll, Autumn." Egon motioned me toward him as he backed up.

Egon the werewolf... normally I'd assume he was stronger but since I'd come from ancient parents and I was a hybrid with the best of both species—and I'd had ancient vampire blood—maybe I'd been underestimating myself all this time. And if I was stronger, maybe I was faster too.

Neither Zack nor I had believed we could do more and therefore hadn't taken advantage of our abilities. I needed to expect more from myself now.

"Can we practice flips, you know like when I'm dodging a hit?" But if I found myself doing stuff that was normally impossible for such a young shape-shifter, how would I explain it to Egon? "Hey, I should probably tell you..."

He relaxed his stance. "Tell me what?"

At the vampire palace, I was given vampire blood. A lot of it. I bit my lip. *I'd be stupid not to take advantage of that. Maybe I'm able to do more than I thought.*

"There's only one way to find out." Egon drew up his fists and pivoted to make himself a smaller target. "And watch out because I won't go easy on you."

He probably had no idea that I'd survived much worse than what he might dish out. I grinned. "And I won't go easy on you either."

"Uh-huh." He regarded me, one eyebrow cocked. "Are you ready?"

"Absolutely," I said. The next instant, he exploded all over me. I rocketed backward and crashed into a wall before he could do more damage.

"Uh, maybe I was a little too cocky before." I groaned, pushing off the floor.

"Possibly." Egon laughed softly. "And though that was rather ungentlemanly of me, Ulric will be far less considerate of your feelings."

"Yeah." I rolled my neck and shoulders. One thing I'd learned from using my supernatural powers was the importance of positive thinking. And being calm. I'd been frustrated when I'd first tried to morph but when I'd finally focused and quit doubting myself, I was able to shift into any form I wanted. Egon's exceptional battle skills had landed him the job as the shape-shifter queen's guard, despite his youth, and that meant something. But I wasn't a lightweight. Maybe I could kick his ass.

"When you're fighting, you have to... how do I explain it?" Egon scratched his chin. "Sometimes it isn't mechanical. Often victory comes from following your instinct. You have to *feel* what your opponent is about to do."

All I had to offer him was a blank look. I mean, I kind of got it but I wasn't sure how to apply that concept.

"Don't just rely on your sight and hearing but other senses as well. Feel the energy around you." He pursed his lips a moment and closed one eye in deep thought. "In order to control anything, you have to be a part of it and let it be a part of you. You have to let it in, and that includes your opponent and their energy. Don't think. Feel."

Yeah... like Dathan had said before, I tended to overthink everything. I needed to *feel* and follow my gut. Whatever power I possessed, I had to tap into it. I needed to own it.

I shut out the noises around me and concentrated on Egon. The sound of his heart beating, the musky scent of his skin, how he shifted his weight from one leg to the other, the rustle of fabric when his hand brushed the cotton of his sweats.

I took in a long slow breath as everyone else in the room fell away. My gaze anchored to his as I felt for his movement. "I'm ready."

He charged me and I spun, landing yards behind him. Then he raced toward me again so fast I didn't see him. Knowing he was coming for me, I vaulted, twirled in the air, and landed behind him again. Closer this time. Before he had a chance to dodge me, I thrust forward, reached around his neck and wrenched the inside of my elbow under his chin.

"Say uncle," I demanded. He coughed as I pressed harder against his Adam's apple. "Say uncle."

"Let him go." Natasha's mouth had flattened into a thin line. I hadn't realized her or the rest of them had stopped to gawk.

After releasing him, I stepped back wondering why

everyone was staring at me like I'd done something wrong. "What?"

"No one but Her Majesty has been able to get Egon in a chokehold." Haji paused to squint at me. "He's too fast and avoiding trouble is his specialty."

I couldn't afford to hold my abilities back for fear that someone would find out I was a weird hybrid. I'd have to roll with whatever and let their minds wander wherever they went. I couldn't worry about any of that, not when our lives were at stake.

I shrugged. "I guess this time I was faster."

Dathan smirked. "Natasha, perhaps you should deal with Autumn and let Egon partner with Haji."

Me spar with an ancient shape-shifter queen with superior fighting skills? She kicked ass even on Dathan, a vampire much older and stronger than her. Damn, just when I'd felt triumphant.

CHAPTER ELEVEN
—— *Zack* ——

WE'D MADE IT through another night without an Ulric invasion. As far as we knew. Months ago, Charles had broken into Autumn's house and remained hidden and healing a full day before finally acting against us. If Ulric managed to break into the compound and had somehow slipped by us through each search, would he show himself right away or hang out a while to assess the situation before attacking?

We were already a half hour into our first training session of the day. War could erupt at any moment and until that time I would stretch my abilities as far as I could get them to go.

As much as I hated being constantly out-maneuvered by Dathan, Autumn had the same problem with Natasha. I caught occasional glimpses of them and each time, Autumn was backtracking to avoid a beating, or she was vaulting up and away. Sometimes when she sprung straight up into the air, it was with Natasha's assistance. I'd never seen anyone strike faster than Natasha and I didn't envy Autumn.

Back at the vampire palace, I'd been forced to train with my dad and I'd hated every minute of it. Sparring with him hadn't gotten any better after my mom had told me he was my not-so-dead father. But that unpleasantness was nothing compared to partnering with Dathan. He was the last person I wanted to go up against in battle. Still, I was grateful for another day to work on my skills.

"You're part vampire, Zack." Dathan blocked my feeble attempt to strike his face. "You're capable of great speed. Use it."

Or maybe not... Maybe this hybrid thing was impossible. I mean, vampires and werewolves were different species. Birds and fish were different species; you didn't see them making hybrids. Maybe vampires and werewolves couldn't mix either. My newly acquired taste for blood could be the result of something else.

A hybrid, me? Seriously? Ridiculous. "Dathan, isn't it possible that my mom was fed vampire blood and that made me crave it for some weird reason?" I huffed. "It doesn't necessarily mean I'm a hybrid."

"Fangs, Zack. Werewolves can't extend them at will, except when they're in their wolf form and even then, they don't change in length."

"Fine, I give up." I raised a palm in surrender. "So how many vampire-werewolf hybrids have you known?"

"None."

"Wait..." I wagged a finger at him. "In a thousand years, you've never met a hybrid like me?"

Dathan shook his head. "No. It was impossible until this past century."

I scratched my head. "How do you figure that?"

He lifted one shoulder and dropped it. "You and Autumn are the only outsiders since the seventeenth century who've been allowed into the inner vampire circle and shown the effect of vampire blood on other species."

"That rare, huh?" Holy crap. "Renzo and my mom didn't know either, yet here I am."

His mouth skewed. "In order to make a hybrid, blood must be stored and kept frozen for months, which wouldn't have been possible until the 19th century when refrigeration was invented." He pursed his mouth in thought. "Or they'd need a vampire captive where they could extract blood on a regular basis."

I nodded, rubbing my chin. "They could capture a vampire, stake him and feed from him for months."

Dathan gave me a smug look. "Female werewolves can't procreate, so the birthing would be left to a human. They'd have to capture a human and get the blood into her system while she's pregnant. Extremely unlikely."

"Improbable, but not impossible."

But his expression told me otherwise. "More likely, the blood would make her and the baby healthier. Remember, your mother was given vampire blood intravenously which a human body processes differently than if it were digested. Intravenous technology was extremely obscure a hundred years ago. Unlikely to have happened before then, especially considering no one, even myself, knew it was even possible."

Wow, I really was a freak.

"And that will remain the reality unless word of your existence gets out. In that case both species will want to kill you while they try to make their own hybrid."

"Right." A freak who was on the run from his own kind but now ran with a dangerous crowd, and could be eliminated simply for being different. Just great.

"Now let's try this maneuver again. I'm going to move rapidly and you're going to stay with me."

Dathan blurred to the other end of the room, weaving through the others sparring. I kept up, staying a fraction of a second behind him.

"Much improved, Zack." He slammed a hand on my shoulder and I wobbled. "We'll do it again. This time, in addition to following me with your eyes, I want you to sense where I am. Follow the energy. Ready?"

I nodded and he vanished out the door toward the stairwell, down the steps and through the underground park. I'd left the area by myself earlier when I first learned I was a hybrid, but both Autumn and my dad had gone after me. We were supposed to go out in groups of four or five. So why was Dathan leading me away from the group?

I followed him past the bench, then beyond the field and caught up with him at the garden patch.

"Nicely done." Dathan's mouth straightened as he studied me. "So... do you love her?"

I wondered how my feelings for Autumn were any business of his. But I was also exploding with curiosity. What the hell was he up to? "Yes. Why?"

"You'd want to be with her even though for the rest of your life you could never truly be with her in the way that a man and woman were meant to be?"

I whistled through my teeth hoping he'd shut the hell up soon. "What's your point, Dathan?"

"As a hybrid, your future together is even more complicated. Don't you think you're being unrealistic?" He sneered. "I find it difficult to believe that you could still see yourself with her a hundred years from now, both of you celibate."

A rumble erupted in my throat and my fangs popped out without my permission. "I swear, Dathan, if you have any plans to break us up..."

He slid a thumb through a belt loop, his gaze steady on mine. "Answer my question."

"I'm never letting Autumn go. A century from now, two centuries, she'll be the only woman I'll ever love." Was he trying to wear me down so I'd give up and he could have Autumn for himself?

Dathan smirked. "You're eighteen, a punk. You have no idea what love is."

"And you have no clue what I think or feel," I snarled. "Lay off, Dathan."

He laughed and the sound reverberated through the park. "You think you can stop me?"

My eyes bulged and the adrenaline roared through my veins. "I'll fight for her. You'd end up having to kill me and then my parents too. And Autumn. Her parents would come after you and if you didn't die then, you'd end up killing your whole army. Who would help you take down Mortimer?"

"Oh, come on, Zack," he said in barely above a whisper. "You think any of them scare me? Not even Mortimer can hurt me and if he stays alive to spread destruction to your kind and Autumn's, that's nothing to me. I'm going after Mortimer because I'm bored."

My limbs trembled. Bored? All this because he had nothing better to do? "So, what, it's all a game to you?"

"Why else would I do all this? You think I care about any of you?" His voice rasped. "And trust me, if I wanted Autumn I'd take her, whether she was willing or not. And there would be nothing you could do about it."

My brain completely shut down and instinct took over. I charged, crashing into him and sending us both across the grassy field. We landed in the bushes. Twigs scraped my face and leaves obscured my view, but I managed to grab a dagger from my back pocket and press it into his neck. "Stay the hell away from her or I'll kill you."

His soft laugh grated over my skin like nuclear waste. "Reacting on your emotions again. What are you going to do now, Zack? Because I'm pretty sure you don't want to kill me. Even if you wanted to, you wouldn't succeed. The fact that you managed to get a knife anywhere near me only means I allowed it."

In my rage, my brain had ceased all rational activity. No way could I get the better of him on my skill alone. Or lack thereof. I'd attacked him and now he could punish me any way he wanted and there wasn't a damn thing I could do about it. Had he set me up? But why? Sweat beaded on my forehead and tickled my skin as it made its way down the side of my face in an agonizingly slow pace.

"Relax, Zack. This was a test. I had to verify your feelings for Autumn. Drill over," he said in the calmest tone I'd ever heard. Was he tricking me? "I'm convinced you'd go to stupid lengths for her, even get yourself killed."

He wasn't going to let me off the hook after I'd attacked him. No way. But what the hell was I supposed to do now? I'd crossed the line, no doubt. I couldn't see this going my way, yet I had no choice but to back off. I flew off of him, stopping at the other end of the field. "Now what?"

"I won't hurt you." He held up both palms toward me. "You have my word."

Dathan always kept his promises. But what if he didn't this time?

"You have to trust me, just as you have these past weeks. I've never led you astray." As he rose from the ground, slowly, he stood and his muscles went lax. "You're fast, Zack, but not fast enough. If I wanted to kill you, you'd already be dead."

When I made like a wax figure and still didn't budge, he rolled his eyes. "Zack, it was a test. I, uh, have something I want to give you but before I let such a valuable piece go, I wanted to make certain it would be for a worthy cause."

All that was a test? And now I really wanted to kill him for putting me through that. While trying to steady my quivering knees, I took a cautious step forward. "You want to *give* me something?" I growled.

Dathan dug into his pocket and revealed a small red velvet box. "It's a ring. Take it."

"So, what, you want me to marry you?" My brows scrunched closer in confusion. "Didn't we already cover my love life? Which I hope would imply my sexual preference."

Dathan's nostrils flared. "This ring was intended for someone I once fancied myself in love with. She gave me hope and that's when I commissioned the ring. That was before I realized what we had wasn't anything close to real love." A storm stirred behind his eyes but quickly passed. "This ring was created out of hope, of which I now have none. But you and Autumn have the chance I never had. Save it for a time when you're ready and then give it to Autumn."

Giving me his almost-wife's wedding ring? There had to be a catch. I lifted the lid and all I saw was a giant sparkly rock the size of my pinky fingernail. I'd never seen such a big diamond except in pictures. I couldn't tell whether the setting was white gold or platinum but it had two smaller diamonds on each side and delicate filigree adorning the band. It had to be worth a small fortune.

"I can't take this." I gently nudged the velvet box away. "It's too much."

"So Autumn isn't worth it?" He sneered.

I scowled. "Don't twist my words."

"Look, I get how much you love her. And I know she loves you back." His top teeth scraped his bottom lip while he hesitated. "Supernaturals mate for life, Zack. And that can be a long time for us. Autumn is your forever."

I could feel the skin puckering between my brows. "Why me?"

"You're not going to make me say it, are you?" Dathan grimaced. "Take the damn ring. Give it to Autumn and create a beautiful life with her."

I bowed back on my heels. "But what are you trying not to say?"

Dathan hissed. "Damn it, Zack, I want you two to be happy together."

So in his strange demented way, Dathan cared about us and wanted us to make our relationship last? Enough to give us a small fortune, apparently. If I didn't take it, would that hurt his feelings? "You think I should go upstairs right now and propose to her?"

"Not necessarily. Hang onto it, if you like. When the time is right, whether it's a month from now or ten years, you'll be ready." Dathan shoved the ring at me.

Keeping my eyes on his in case this was a trick, I gingerly relieved him of the small velvet box. I would definitely be giving Autumn a ring one day and this one was stunning. Plus, why not a big sparkly one that screamed to everyone she was already taken? No guy could miss that thing on her finger. The more I thought about giving Autumn the ring, the more I wanted to.

And I would—assuming that we survived the battle with Ulric and then King Mortimer. "Thank you."

"You're welcome. One more thing."

I inwardly cringed. I felt another ambush coming on. "What?"

"You and I can do things others here can't. If we find ourselves under attack, and for whatever reason don't want to kill our opponent, feed from him instead. Once you make that physical contact, you can command him to stand down."

I couldn't imagine Ulric or one of his men attacking and me not needing to maim him. "Wouldn't stopping for a snack slow me down?"

Dathan gripped my shoulders. "Very soon, you may be confronted with an attacker who's actually your friend. Just remember what I said. Once your fangs penetrate their skin, they become numb and dazed. They won't even remember you feeding from them, if you command them not to. They won't see any bite marks either because our saliva heals the wound almost instantly." Dathan paused. "But I digress. Best to use words, not thoughts. And remember that the unconscious mind is literal and will follow all commands exactly. Be careful what you tell them and say only what you absolutely have to."

Dathan didn't dole out unnecessary advice. If he thought I'd end up in battle with someone I didn't want to hurt, then I probably would. "Got it."

We entered the training area again and Autumn immediately zoomed over. She touched my shoulder, her eyes scanning the length of me for any damage. "Are you okay?"

"Shouldn't you be asking your fiancé?" Dathan butted in. "I'm the one who got attacked."

"What?" Autumn's voice took on a hint of hysteria. "Did Ulric or one of his men get in here?"

"None of the above." Dathan aimed an index finger at me. "This guy got a little angry and violent while we were sparring."

"Uh-huh." She squinted, glancing from me to Dathan. "I'm betting you provoked him."

Dathan threw his head back and laughed, then returned to the spot where we'd been sparring. That was my cue to get busy.

I'll fill you in later, I told Autumn. Obviously, I'd have to omit big chunks of the incident, especially anything that involved the ring or my feelings for her.

After a couple hours of hardcore training, Yvonne and Sean strolled in. "You called, Your Majesty?" he asked, as about half the compound's inhabitants poured into the training area.

"Yes." Natasha swept toward them. "I want to do an aerial inspection, see if we can locate Ulric or any nearby werewolves. If we know his whereabouts, perhaps we can decrease our chances of being caught off guard."

"If an aerial search is conducted, you should be excluded, Your Majesty," Sean said, his eyes fierce.

Yvonne grunted. "Agreed. I'm sorry, Your Majesty, but we can't allow you on such a mission."

Silence permeated the room like electricity, charging the air with tension. Pretty ballsy outright disobeying the queen. The last thing we needed right now was mutiny.

CHAPTER TWELVE
——— *Autumn* ———

NATASHA'S BLUE EYES glinted like cobalt. "Last time I checked, I was the shape-shifter queen. *I* give the orders."

"Yes," Sean agreed. "And per *your* orders, I must keep you safe. You will stay here while others go in your stead."

When Natasha opened her mouth, Yvonne cut her off. "As your loyal subject sworn to allegiance, I'm afraid I must agree with Sean."

"I'll go, Your Majesty." Persius powered through the throng of people to stand beside Yvonne and Sean. "Three more and we have a full team."

"I'll go too," Haji added. "Maybe we form another team and cover more ground faster."

"I'm in," came a shout from the crowd.

Natasha's voice was drowned out with a chorus of volunteers. Her eyebrows drawn, she zeroed in on my father. He nodded and her shoulders slumped. I didn't have to wonder why Natasha was listening to my dad now—her older brother.

Interesting dynamics between Natasha and your father, don't you think? Dathan spoke into my head. *Did you get the rest of the story from him?*

I located Dathan sitting in a nearby chair and shrugged, not feeling the need to tell him I already had the info.

Well, no need to rush the rest of the truth. It won't change the path of our war.

It's all about the war for you, isn't it? I sent him a scathing look. *Sometimes I wonder if you care about anyone besides yourself.*

My dear, Autumn, he said, rising from his chair. *I was blissfully ignorant until you came along. If not for you and your friends, I'd still be sleeping comfortably.* He stalked toward me. *If I didn't care, I'd be at my palace right now. If I didn't care, I would've let you and Zack go on being blind to what you are. If I didn't care, I wouldn't be here.* He loomed over me, his eyes on fire. *You started all of this and now you're going to help me finish it.*

The noise around me increased, but I was too focused on Dathan to allow the ruckus to fully register.

"Problem?" Zack's gaze bounced from me to Dathan.

I told myself to breathe. In and then out. I'd been wondering what Dathan's ulterior motive was, but now I believed there wasn't one. He just had sneaky ways of going about accomplishing the plan I already knew about.

"No." I brushed my shoulder against Zack so he could hear what I was about to say to Dathan. *We* need to break up because sooner or later, someone's going to notice these little moments between the three of us. You don't need me anymore; you already got acceptance from everyone here. And our breakup needs to be public, for obvious reasons._

Dathan groaned. *Whatever you say. I'll trust you to choose the right moment.* "If you'll excuse me, I need to pay attention." He flipped around to tune in to the crowd.

Natasha eyes dulled as she seemed to relent, directing her words at Yvonne and Sean. "Fine. I will take your advice and reluctantly give my consent for my people to put themselves at risk."

A collective sigh whispered through the shape-shifters, including me. She was my aunt and my parents cared deeply for her. I needed her to be safe.

"I'll be one of the twenty," my dad volunteered. "We brought Ulric to you. We can't let your people take the biggest risks."

Natasha waved her hand at my dad as if erasing everything he'd said. "No. My people know the area and we can do it more efficiently. You will stay here with Olivia and your daughter. Ensure that the young are as ready for battle as they can be."

My limbs sagged in relief. It's not like my dad could defy his queen.

"I need all volunteers to coordinate with me now," Sean said.

As the shape-shifters gathered around Sean, I gravitated toward Renzo and Zack while I watched my parents. Their eyes were glued to Natasha, their brows scrunched in worry—probably because we could lose some of the crew. Hell, maybe more than just some. We had no idea how many uber powerful werewolves Ulric had with him or what they had planned for us.

Even as my chest tightened at the unknown and possible death toll, I knew we didn't have a choice but to proceed with the aerial search.

CHAPTER THIRTEEN
—— *Zack* ——

WITH NOTHING BETTER to do while Natasha and Sean organized their volunteers, I slanted against the wall and snuck occasional glances at Autumn who was whispering with her mom. Dathan chatted to Quentin.

Watch this. Autumn's eyes flashed.

"Dathan." She spoke loudly, like she wasn't trying to be discreet. "I need to talk to you."

Dathan's eyes narrowed and guarded. "What is it, sugar?" he asked, rising from his chair.

I inched closer to them so I didn't miss anything. Olivia stood too, as though protective over her daughter.

"You probably shouldn't call me that anymore." She angled her chin toward her chest, her eyes wide and filled with regret. "I can't marry you, Dathan. I'm so sorry."

A harsh laugh escaped him. "Oh, you can't, huh? And why is that?"

"A lot of reasons. I mean, you're plenty attractive, but I feel like we don't really connect anymore, you know?"

I couldn't help but grin.

"I understand." He bit his bottom lip, and I wasn't sure if he was suppressing his amusement. "Is there someone else?" *You're welcome, Zack.*

"Uh..." She scanned the dead-silent enthralled audience—who were all waiting to see how the disengagement unfolded. "There's someone I've been getting closer to. Which is why it's not fair to you if I continue this. It feels wrong to commit to one person when I can't stop thinking about someone else."

"Well, I can't deny that we've been drifting apart. This is probably for the best," Dathan muttered. "Are you going to tell me who it is or shall I guess? You have my word that no harm will come to him." He followed the path of her gaze, then scoffed. "Zack? You'd rather be with a commoner than a vampire king? I guess you two are perfect for each other."

Thank you, I told him as he headed for the stairwell.

No sweat. He halted, pivoted and surveyed the room. *We're basically done for a while. If you're smart, you'll both escape into the queen's apartment before it gets crowded. Go now and I'll escort you.*

I don't have to be told twice, I pushed into his head, then focused on Autumn. *Meet me in our room?*

You go first, she answered. *I'll slip out as soon as everyone stops staring.*

My clever girl just paved the way so we didn't have to hide. I could get a proper kiss from her. In front of everyone. Maybe not this second, but as soon as a respectable amount of time had passed. I imagined the possibilities and smiled to myself.

Dathan and I waited in the hallway for Autumn, then the three of us dashed down the stairs to the next floor. At the door to Natasha's suite, I let the security system scan my eyes. The door glided sideways and Autumn and I hurried through.

I'll be in the park, sulking over how I've been jilted. If you two decide to go anywhere, let me know and I'll be back to escort you. Dathan saluted us as the door slid shut.

Thanks, I said.

Autumn wrapped herself around me like a blanket. I staggered over to the sofa, pulling her down and adjusting her in my lap. Her hands weaved through my hair and her mouth covered mine, swallowing my moan. I pressed her closer until her torso flattened against mine.

I didn't get very far. I'm right outside the door with Olivia and Quentin, Dathan told me. *I won't be able to delay them but another minute or two.*

Frustration consumed me and I did the opposite of everything I wanted to do. I nudged Autumn back, then gripped her hips as I stood. Her legs slid down the length of me and I stifled the urge to rush to the door and somehow reinforce it so no one could get to us.

Autumn leaned into me with her chin tilted up, tangling her fingers through mine. She was so damn cute when she looked at me like that. I landed a kiss on her forehead as her parents barged in. "What's up, Mom?" she asked.

"I was worried so I followed your scent. It's dangerous for you two to be alone, even here." Olivia scanned the room. "There's no security system that can't be hacked, no fort that can hold forever."

I tried not to think about what Autumn's parents probably assumed I'd been doing with their daughter. Quentin seemed friendly enough but Olivia always kept her distance. I wondered what about me—other than the fact that I wanted to violate her daughter—made her dislike me so much. Was she still prejudiced against werewolves? Or did she dislike me even more now that she knew I was also part vampire?

Autumn plopped down on the couch, dragging me with her. "Is there news?" she asked.

"Natasha wants them to wait until morning after they've had a chance to rest and feed. Sixteen of them will split into four groups so they can cover more ground and finish faster." Quentin scratched his chin. "Unfortunately, nine others have decided they don't want to die in a battle they believe we can't possibly win. That leaves about twenty staying behind."

"They believe we can't win?" Autumn gripped my hand. "That's disturbing."

"I agree," Olivia answered. "The deserters will fly out with the scouting teams through the skylight. The ones who've declared themselves out of the fight won't be allowed back in."

"The deserters should be shot," Dathan grumbled.

"Actually, I'm surprised all of them aren't deserting," Quentin mumbled.

Autumn studied her father. "Why do you look so worried?"

Natasha swept into the living room, followed by my dad. "Worried about what?" she asked.

"Once they leave in the morning, the remaining shifters aren't your strongest fighters," Quentin said. "A couple of them work the kitchen, one or two keep the gardens, another handles building maintenance and the rest are the scientists from the research department. Except for Yvonne and Sean, none of them are warriors."

"The least skilled fighters," Dathan said. "Which means while the others are scouting for Ulric, we're essentially alone."

"Not necessarily." Natasha's face appeared drawn and tired. "They may not be as experienced as you or me, but they still have considerable training. Everyone here trains. I guess it's for the best that the others are leaving. We've lost so many battles over the centuries so I don't blame them. But those with little faith will only hold us back."

"Hang on," I said. "We're all warriors; seven of us here in this room. And as Natasha pointed out, the remaining crew has trained. We might be stressing out over nothing. We have a good chance against a few crazy werewolves."

Olivia paced the other end of the room, keeping a safe distance from my dad and me, as usual. "It's probably not only a few, Zack. There may be ten or more men with him. At least."

"And they're all amped up on vampire blood." Quentin pinned me with a stare, then turned to Autumn. "If those psychos manage to get inside this place, we need to be together to fight them."

"Otherwise, they can pick us off, one by one," Renzo added. *Sorry, bud. You'll have time for Autumn when this is all over.*

How much longer could Autumn and I keep this up and still have a relationship? My mood deflated like an empty blood bag.

CHAPTER FOURTEEN
──────── *Autumn* ────────

THE NEXT MORNING, all the compound residents gathered around Natasha and Sean. Havers and Kieran had already checked the exterior monitors with extra diligence but Natasha wanted one person to go outside and make double sure she wasn't sending her entire scouting party to the slaughter. Natasha tried to be that one person, but Sean and Yvonne shot her down. Not only did Sean volunteer to do the initial perimeter scope, he insisted on it.

"I don't like you going out there alone." Natasha's mouth turned down as Sean prepared to shift into a bird and exit through the skylight.

"Someone has to." Sean patted his pocket, pulled out a wallet then stuffed it back in. At least if he ended up being out too long, he had a leather wallet which would morph with him. "I won't risk my queen's life or anyone else's. Besides, so long as I stay in the air, I'm safe."

"Not necessarily." Dathan clamped a hand on Sean's shoulder. "As soon as you pass through the skylight, I want a connection with you. Talk or hum to me and don't stop until you return. If you stop, I'll assume our connection was interrupted by Ulric."

Sean cast a doubtful glance at Dathan. "Because you think Ulric is capable of glamouring me from hundreds of feet away. And that's assuming he realizes I'm a shifter."

"Do as he says, Sean." Natasha's eyes pooled as she gave his arm a squeeze. "And be careful."

"I will." His arms vibrated for an instant before he morphed into an eagle. His majestic wings flapped, taking him higher and higher until he reached the ceiling. The skylight glided open and his wings whispered past the glass, then it closed after him.

With Sean gone, silence engulfed the room as we all waited. Dathan wandered to a corner, pensive as he tuned in telepathically to Sean.

I nibbled on my cuticles and glanced around the room, my attention frequently returning to the skylight above. Sean had to stay safe. And once all sixteen of them were gone, I needed every single one to survive. We could fight the upcoming battle without them, but as much as I wanted to think positively, I needed to be practical. The smaller our army, the less our chances of winning. Plus, they were good people and didn't deserve to be murdered. Though my head told me Sean would be fine, my gut warned me to prepare for anything.

"When Sean returns with news that the area is secure, how long do you think they'll be out scouting?" I asked Natasha.

"Days." Dad materialized at my side. "Shape-shifters usually fly as common birds that travel in flocks, like ducks or pigeons. They'll draw less attention but travel slower."

"They'll zigzag to cover more ground and that will slow them down," my mom added. "Plus, they'll need to stop occasionally to rest or refuel."

Days? Fluttering above had our eyes riveted to the ceiling. The hatch opened and Sean glided down, the breeze from his wings reaching me and lifting my hair. As soon as his feet touched the floor, he morphed back into his human form. "The mountain is clear. We should leave right away."

"Don't forget to check in every hour or so," Natasha reminded him.

The team of sixteen said their goodbyes, then morphed into pigeons. The hatch opened again, they flew through the small opening at the ceiling and then the glass slid over after them. As I stood there staring up, Zack draped an arm around my shoulders and drew me against him. "They'll be okay. They've all been around a while and they're smart."

The full scope of the mission hit me just then and my stomach bottomed out. "They won't always be up in the sky untouchable. Each time they stop to eat or rest, they could be discovered and captured. And if they don't find Ulric, they stay out longer..." My voice trailed off.

My dad's mouth set into a grim line. "The longer they're out, the higher the risk of Ulric discovering them."

What could I say to that? We could lose a major portion of our army, but we'd allowed them to leave anyway. And maybe none of them were related to me, but they were loved by someone. Each one of them mattered. "They shouldn't have gone."

"Yes, this was an extremely bad idea." Dathan glanced up at the skylight. "We can't keep tabs on all of them at every second. Ulric could get power over one of them at any moment and we won't know. We should call them back."

Natasha's gaze snapped to Dathan. "We can't. We need to find Ulric and this is the only way. Otherwise, we're sitting ducks waiting to be picked off."

Dathan knocked his fist against the wall and dust floated in the air. "I don't know what pisses me off more—that you're right or that I couldn't come up with a better way."

"Practice without me. I have some business to attend to." Natasha's eyes fluttered before she disappeared through the door.

Dathan snapped his fingers at Yvonne and a couple others. "Follow her."

They rocketed out the door after Natasha. A few other shape-shifters and a couple werewolves scurried off too, leaving Zack and me with Dathan, my parents and Renzo.

"War is never pretty, sweetheart. Sacrifices will always be made." My dad jerked his head toward the training room. "Let's make this time count."

I trained with my mom and practiced escaping

serious damage to my body, while Zack sparred with Renzo. When the delicious aroma coming from the kitchen became too much, we headed to the private dining room. Once I'd gotten dibs on the chair next to Zack, I scooted closer to him. *I don't know about you but I'm scared. I'm going to spend every spare second training.*

He rotated toward me, ran a palm up my arm and down again. *Me too. As much as I want to sneak somewhere with you, especially now that everyone knows you're not engaged, we can't afford to lose focus.*

My heart squeezed, then shattered, at how easily he'd abandoned any thoughts of private time together. And whether I should've been disturbed or not, I couldn't help but be afraid we'd somehow drift apart. My eyes stung and I shifted away.

"Autumn." He cupped my face with both hands. "Something wrong?"

I squirmed in my chair. "Just... out of sight, out of mind."

He laughed once. "That didn't work when I was actually trying to forget about you and it certainly won't work now."

On impulse, I swayed toward him and brushed his lips with my own. "Pinky swear?"

"Easiest pinky swear I've ever made." He looped his little finger around mine, then yanked me closer, dropping a kiss on the tip of my nose.

I knew he believed what he said. I just didn't think either of us could predict the future. Unfortunately, even if we survived Ulric and we triumphed over King Mortimer, our relationship stood little chance of surviving. Even if Zack truly loved me, his feelings for me weren't enough to overcome so many obstacles. And if he loved me, wouldn't he have told me so by now?

† † †

Since Natasha was preoccupied with Queen duties, I trained with my mom the next day too. Sean checked in periodically but still no sign of Ulric. With each passing hour, I felt more ready for battle. But with each report that arrived with no news, I grew more scared. Maybe they couldn't find Ulric or his men because he was in the tunnel again.

"How long before they give up the search?" I asked my dad when we broke for dinner.

"If it were me..." He piled his fork with more scalloped potatoes. "I wouldn't stay out longer than a day or so."

"If they return without locating Ulric, I'll go after him myself," Dathan said. "I'll make a lot of noise so he can't help but see me coming. I'll be ready for him."

I shook my head, nerves raw and my knees vibrating. "You have no way of knowing if you'll get to him before he gets to us."

Dathan grinned. "Keep training, sugar."

"Don't make me hurt you, Dathan," Zack growled.

Dathan grew more amused, his eyes twinkling.

After dinner, Renzo trained with Dathan while my mom and dad coerced us to the park to train. My dad thrust a bow at Zack for archery lessons, and my mom retrieved a bunch of throwing knives from her back pocket. One knife looked like someone would use it on steak and I was pretty sure I spotted a screwdriver.

She held out a blade with the handle pointing in my direction, then set the others on a nearby picnic table. I stared at the eight-inch blade a moment before facing the target. I grasped the handle firmly and threw it at the chunk of wood. It bounced off the edge, landing nowhere near the center.

She blinked, then frowned. "You've obviously spent very little time throwing knives."

"If you had asked me, I could've told you that," I grumbled.

My mom chuckled and snatched up one of the knives. She demonstrated the correct way to throw one, then I gave it a shot. We practiced for the next hour and much to my astonishment, I was hitting the targets usually within a couple of inches.

I paused to glance over at Zack who was stretching a bow. He released the arrow which landed several yards away on the edge of the stump.

I plucked a screwdriver from the pile of knives, brought my opposite side foot forward like she'd taught me, then flung the screwdriver at the target. It stuck.

"Nicely done." She beamed. "Works the same for ice picks or whatever pointy object you can find."

"Ready to switch?" my dad asked, planting a kiss on my mom's forehead.

I wondered if my mom would give Zack knife throwing lessons and risk him sniffing her out. I didn't have to wonder long. In several long strides, my dad had covered the distance and was retrieving the blades from the target I'd been using. A glance to where they'd been working revealed all the equipment they'd been using. Waiting for us. Nope, my mom wouldn't be working with Zack and she wouldn't be revealing her true self today.

I wanted to tell Zack about my mom, that mixing species was all a bunch of crap King Mortimer had conjured up so no one would ever again try what Hannah and Eli had. But I'd promised my mom to keep it a secret. And I intended on keeping that promise if it killed me.

CHAPTER FIFTEEN

—— *Autumn* ——

THE NEXT MORNING, my patience was as strained as a tightrope. I had nothing to ground me, no net below to catch me. Natasha's scouts had been gone a full forty-eight hours. Wherever that crazy bastard Ulric was hiding, we wouldn't find him until he wanted us to.

Silence filled the dining area except for the occasional clanging of kitchenware as Ivan and Valerie brought over plates of scrambled eggs, hash browns and sausage.

"Thank you." Dathan took the plate of eggs and loaded his fork, then focused on Natasha. "Any word from your men?"

"Not yet this morning, but I'll try one of them now." Natasha stared down at her hashed browns as energy swirled around the table.

I stabbed a piece of sausage, contemplating whether or not I should turn carnivore.

Zack bumped me with his shoulder. "No point in holding out anymore," he said. "You don't need to hide your scent here."

Except that if my scent became stronger, I might smell more like a werewolf, not a shape-shifter. That would bring attention to my parents and who they were. "True. But one day, we won't be secluded inside this place and I'll encounter other werewolves. Might be convenient for me to be able to pass as a human." Swallowing the excess saliva that had pooled in my mouth, I nudged the sausage over to Zack's plate.

"They're heading back now," Natasha said. "It'll be a few hours since Rakin's group made it all the way to Bishop. Haji and his group are coming from Sacramento and they might circle a few miles around the compound first."

"They're safe, all of them?" I asked.

"So far, so good." Natasha finished off her eggs and nudged the plate away.

Just as my muscles relaxed one by one, Dathan tossed a crumpled napkin on the table. "If Ulric or his gang are in the tunnel or outside waiting for your men, the trick will be reentering without Ulric sneaking in with them."

"We'll be watching when they come in," Natasha added. Despite her even delivery of the words, worry lines marred her flawless skin. "But we should all be ready for battle anyway."

"Or maybe Ulric will strike before the rest of our army returns." Dathan's lip twisted. "That's what I'd do. Less people to fight."

Zack angled his head, then pushed away from the table. "He'd have to get in, which we don't think he's managed so far."

"You're forgetting about Lulu." Dathan expelled his breath sharply. "Ulric's been at this game for centuries. The hunt is his favorite part, scoping out the area, solving problems and waiting for the right moment."

I stretched in an attempt to relax a muscle cramp that had formed while Dathan had been sucking away our hope. "So you think he's definitely been inside and is probably here right now?"

Dathan studied each face at the table then tipped back in his chair. "I believe Ulric's powers have evolved to hypnotize someone to gain complete control. For all we know, our entire army may arrive and no longer be our army at all."

"You keep talking about his power to hypnotize, but you have no evidence." My dad stood then paced the small dining room.

"I've repeated myself because you all keep discounting it," Dathan replied in a clipped voice. "Just because you don't want to believe something doesn't make it not so."

My dad scrubbed his face with his palms. "I know. I'm just frustrated."

"We're not ignoring your theory, Dathan. It's just that we don't even know how to fight someone with that kind of power." Renzo squinted, his mouth twisted. "You think that Ulric could control the older ones like us?"

"Probably not." Dathan paused, staring off in thought. "But we should be prepared for the possibility that he could have control over our younger, less strong crew. For instance, the two we lost a few days ago could have given him the information he wanted."

"If so, we're no longer safe here." My mom's gaze snapped from Renzo to Dathan and back to my dad. "We should go."

"Because it's safer out there?" Dathan bolted from the chair to tower over my mom. "If, in theory, Ulric was somewhere nearby, couldn't he already have set traps? You wouldn't get far."

The back of my neck tingled with the sense that Ulric was close. My adrenaline spiked through my fingertips, making them tremble. "I'm with Dathan. Whatever Ulric has planned is already in motion. If we run, we're falling right into his trap."

"This is a lot of speculation." Renzo tapped his short nails against the tabletop. "I think we should wait until we hear from Sean and Haji and the rest, then regroup."

"That's the plan." Natasha wiped her mouth with a napkin. "And we're sticking to it."

Dathan strode to the doorway, gesturing toward the sparring area, then he disappeared from my view, along with my parents. I sprinted to catch up with them. "Mom, can we work with knives again? I also want to practice with swords."

"Sure." My mom waved Zack and me past the training area toward the park.

"Great." I much preferred training with my parents than Dathan. I spun around to send him a smug smile and nearly bumped into him.

"I think we should make this interesting." Dathan smirked as he sidestepped to avoid crashing into me, and ventured farther into the park.

Ugh. I already wasn't looking forward to whatever he had in mind. Hoping Dathan would go away, I set up the wood board for target practice while Zack gathered the blades.

My mom crossed her arms over her chest and, by her expression, her thoughts matched mine. "I don't think we have the same definition of interesting."

Dathan snickered. "They've been working with a hunk of wood that never moves. Ulric and his men will be mobile and they've had plenty of practice avoiding knives."

I doubted Dathan was suggesting we target practice on him. I groaned. "No. I'm not going to throw weapons at my family."

"Of course not. They've already paid their dues. But if you refuse to throw things at Zack, then he can throw things at you instead." His eyes sparkled and his mouth twitched.

That didn't sound any better. Sparring was one thing. Slicing and dicing which drew blood was quite another. When I opened my mouth to object, I realized neither of my parents had beaten me to it. My attention bounced between the two of them. "You don't think this is a good idea, do you?"

"Well..." My mom lifted her shoulders. "You both need practice hitting your mark and avoiding being staked or knifed."

Dad sent me an apologetic smile. "As much as I hate the thought of you getting hurt, honey, it makes sense. You'll both heal quickly enough."

I flinched, revulsion brewing in my gut. "You want Zack and me to try to maim each other?"

"Sweetheart," my mom said in a soothing voice. "We've all been in your position and we already took turns being targets. It's like a rite of passage for any great warrior."

"A skilled warrior has a better chance of survival. That's what we all want, right?" my dad asked, pinching my cheek.

Oh, just great. If I followed their advice, I'd be using my boyfriend for target practice, drawing blood. Each time we aimed, we'd be torn between getting a bull's-eye and knifing each other or missing the target and not improving our warrior skills.

I could hardly wait.

"Now that the game rules have changed, three of us aren't necessary. I'll take care of them," Dathan told my parents as he hooked a thumb into his belt loop.

He was staying to watch over us? I moaned and let my head fall back.

"You're in good hands, sweetheart." My dad cupped my chin and planted a kiss on my forehead.

I wasn't sure which turned my stomach more—Zack and I stalking each other with intent to damage one another or knowing Dathan and his twisted mind would enjoy watching us struggle with the process. He'd better not gloat when Zack and I succeeded at hurting each other.

Thirty minutes later, I'd hit Zack once in his thigh and once in the back—not my proudest moments. I'd started with five knives and missed hitting him once. I had two left. Anticipating what Zack would do next was tricky since his vampire speed required me to already have thrown the knife before he got to the spot. But my instinct with Zack was pretty good.

Zack stopped behind the protection of a thick tree trunk. He inched to the left and became visible, but the toe on his other side pointed in the opposite direction. He was trying to fake me out. His foot shifted and I threw, shooting for his midsection. It sank into his side and Zack yanked it out before rocketing out of my vision.

One more knife left. How I loathed having to hunt Zack like he were my prey. I couldn't have been more finished with this drill.

His scent was everywhere, so I couldn't rely on my nose to find him. And I didn't hear a thing which meant he was holding his breath. If he was mobile, he was extremely quiet about it. All I could do now was search for Zack's energy, feel where he was. Following my instinct and trusting my connection to him, I dashed to a shed near the edge of the park. His scent was a hint stronger.

I'm sorry, Zack.

Yeah, I hate this. But we can't afford to waste time. You'll probably be sorrier when I'm the one holding the knives.

I've got one more left, I told him creeping closer to the shed. *Let's get it over with.*

I'm not going to make it easy for you, if that's what you mean. Especially when you might miss your next shot.

Now I *knew* where he was hiding since he emitted energy while we spoke telepathically. Which meant if I answered Zack, he'd realize I was almost right behind him.

Fabric rustled which told me Zack was likely getting ready to bolt. Standing as still as the shed he was creeping around, I waited. My ears picked up the tiniest sound of his boots creaking. As soon as he rounded the corner, I leapt onto him. I wrapped myself around him and nuzzled my nose against the pocket at his shoulder and neck.

He stiffened, probably expecting me to shove a knife into him. After a moment, he relaxed against me as his warm hands slid around my waist and up my spine. "I expected to get stabbed, not this."

I planted a kiss at his throat. "Yeah, me too."

"Back to work," Dathan hissed.

Zack released me, rolling his eyes at Dathan. "Let's switch now."

I offered him the unused blade, knowing he still had the three I'd thrown at him. If he found the one that hadn't hit him, he'd have five. Maybe I'd find it first and save myself an extra wound.

Leaning toward him, I lifted my chin. He kissed me and lingered an instant before I took advantage of his guard being down, and vanished.

Nice, he laughed into my head.

And don't try locating me through telepathic energy, because I won't be talking to you until after this drill is over. Later, babe.

Turns out, Zack didn't need to track my energy to catch up to me. He was faster. Yay me. Despite his speed though, he missed one out of four shots, like I had. Or maybe that was because he couldn't bring himself to do worse to me than I did to him.

"Good job, Zack. Getting her in the back of the knee was pure genius." Dathan slapped Zack on the shoulder. "Slowed her down long enough for you to get the next one in her neck."

He'd also hit me in the shoulder. Well, maybe Zack did do worse to me than I had done to him.

Sorry, he mouthed to me.

"Let's put you two on swords." Dathan gestured toward the door leading us out of the park.

"Against each other again?" Zack asked, his tone strained.

"Of course. Let's get our weapons."

Zack and I groaned at the same time, but returned with Dathan to the training area. We found Natasha sparring with my mom, and Renzo sparring with my dad. They all stopped when they spotted us.

My mom scowled at the blood around the hole in my T-shirt. "I see Zack's aim has improved."

I hitched a thumb at Zack's side. "So has mine."

"Sorry about that, hon." My mom stroked my arms. "But we don't have time to be nice and the best way to learn is by doing. If you'd practiced with your father or me, you'd never hit us. If we were gunning for you, you'd never get away."

"It's okay," Zack told her. "She and I got through it. And it freed you guys up to do other things."

"And you have more time since they're about to cut each other up with swords." Dathan smirked.

Just great. I'd try not to chop off my boyfriend's arm.

We chose our swords, and headed back to the park. After an hour swinging at Zack and trying to avoid getting shredded, I tossed my sword in the air in frustration. Gravity took over and the blade plummeted, twirled, and then the tip sank into the grass.

"A definite improvement," Dathan said, raising a brow at the sword sticking straight up out of the ground.

Although I could tell the difference too, I wasn't nearly skilled enough to win a battle against Ulric. But I'd annoy him and make things much more difficult than he might expect. Maybe keep him busy long enough for help to arrive.

In any case, I was done with swords for the day. "I'm tired of attacking my boyfriend. If you don't mind, let's do something else."

"Fair enough." Dathan slanted his head toward the park exit.

Back in the training room, my dad stopped his assault on Renzo and my mom stepped away from Natasha, sweat beading over their neck and chests. They had to be capable of doing some serious damage to Ulric. Too bad Ulric would probably have plenty of friends with him.

"Any word from the crew?" I asked Natasha.

"No one has checked in for well over an hour." Natasha's top teeth worried her bottom lip. "In theory, some of the crew should have already arrived."

"They're MIA?" Renzo grated out.

"Not sure. I tried Sean again a few minutes ago." The muscle in her jaw flexed. "Actually, I've tried them all. Nothing yet."

Crap. This was not good news.

CHAPTER SIXTEEN
—— *Autumn* ——

"WHEN WAS THE last time you heard from Sean?" I asked, my voice rising in pitch. I dragged in a long slow breath in an attempt to appear calmer. I didn't want to be the cause of everyone in the compound becoming more panicked.

"Well over an hour ago." Natasha bowed her head a moment, then lifted her chin. "It could be anything delaying him. If a werewolf is nearby, talking telepathically will draw attention to them. I imagine he'll answer shortly."

"But you could sense if anything's happened to them, yeah?" I asked.

"They're alive, as near as I can tell. Connection's weak though." Natasha pursed her lips.

Renzo sighed. "Telepathic connections usually get weaker with decreased consciousness."

The blue in Natasha's eyes deepened as she stared at Renzo a beat, then she glanced away. "Lunch is ready." Without another word, she strode toward the cafeteria.

We sat in our usual spots, Natasha occasionally glancing to Sean's empty place. Silence pervaded the room, each of us lost in our own thoughts—or worst fears. Tension oozed from each of us until it permeated the space and my stomach churned. I'd nearly forced down all my lunch when air rushed from Natasha's lungs.

"Oh, thank God. They're waiting at the skylight now. Havers, they're here. Do another check on the monitors around the skylight before letting them in." She dropped her fork and rushed to the atrium.

The rest of us abandoned our breakfast and scurried after her. Natasha bit her lip as she stood in the atrium and looked up. Metal slid to the side, exposing the skylight. Shadows flittered over the glass above.

"Havers, is it safe?" Natasha muttered as her gaze remained locked above. "Go ahead and open it."

"Keep watch for anyone else trying to crash our party," Dathan said. "Don't take your eyes off the skylight until they're all inside and we've closed up."

The glass moved and Zack stiffened at my side. My fingers curled around his while my other hand felt for the handles of the throwing knives I'd begun hiding in my waistband.

The sound of flapping wings ripped through the room as pigeons descended. When the birds neared the floor, they shifted to human. I did a quick head count. Twelve.

"Where are the other four?" Natasha demanded.

"They were still too far away and I was uncomfortable leaving the rest of my men exposed out there for so long. I imagine they'll be here any minute." Sean sniffed the air. "Smells like breakfast. We're starving."

Natasha nodded toward the cafeteria. "Let's get you refueled."

The twelve shape-shifters sped into the dining area. Energy swirled and I traced it to Dathan who was staring intently at Natasha.

She scowled and after a few moments huffed. "Fine. If it will make you happy."

"None of this makes me happy, angel. Of all people, you should know that." Dathan fired off a stern look before glancing over his shoulder. "Autumn and Zack, come with me."

What's going on? Zack asked, still hanging onto me as we sprinted to keep up with Dathan.

The scouting crew, every single one of them, will need to be observed until we're absolutely certain their minds haven't been tampered with in any way. Dathan pushed the door open to the cafeteria and made a beeline to the buffet. Sean didn't turn around and all I could see was the back of his short light brown hair.

"Good to have you back safely, Sean."

"Hey, Dathan," Sean said, glancing over his beefy shoulder as he heaped a generous portion of mashed potatoes onto his plate. "Need something?"

"I have questions." Dathan leaned against the wall, casually scrutinizing everyone in the room. "At any time, did any of your crew fall off the radar?"

"No." Sean moved to the next dish and grabbed tongs to poke through the steaks. "I kept in constant contact with them. If anything happened, I'd know."

"Natasha didn't hear from you for nearly an hour. What happened during that time?" Dathan stepped out of the way as one of the other guys headed to the table with a full plate.

"We hadn't slept since we left. I wanted to make sure that when we arrived, we were alert enough to deal with anything." Sean spooned butternut squash onto his plate. "We had a power nap not too far from here."

"Of course." Dathan's eyes narrowed. "None of you encountered Ulric anywhere during the whole mission?"

Sean leaned away from the buffet and straightened his spine. "If I saw Ulric, I would've reported it. Same with the rest of the crew."

"Who were the other three with you?"

Sean blinked. "Steven, Rosa and Tiffany."

"And where are the missing four?" Dathan fired off.

"They're not missing. In fact, they should be arriving any second." Sean tipped his head toward his plate. "We haven't had a decent meal in a while and we're all exhausted."

"Eat and rest." Dathan's shoulders relaxed as he offered Sean a smile. "Take care of your crew. You've all earned it."

Following Dathan's lead, Zack and I exited the cafeteria and returned to the atrium where Natasha, my parents and Renzo were waiting for the last four to arrive.

What did you get from all that? I asked Dathan.

Not as much as I had hoped. Yet more than I wanted. He seemed to mull over his next words. *I need to speak with you and Zack. In private.*

"They're here." Natasha peered up at the skylights.

The glass above slid open and four pigeons flapped their wings as they lowered, then morphed into humans inches before reaching the floor. Natasha greeted them warmly, and whisked them off to the cafeteria to refuel.

"I'm taking the kids with me to patrol the area," Dathan called out.

Knowing Zack and I were "the kids," we trailed after him as he headed for the stairwell. Before the heavy metal door, he surveyed the vicinity. Zack and I did too.

My mom caught up to us, as if sensing Dathan was up to no good. "I'll come with you. I need to ensure my daughter doesn't encounter Ulric with only you to protect her."

"Five is better than four." My dad appeared and draped an arm over my mom's shoulders. "I can make sure both my girls stay alive."

Renzo joined the circle. "Six is better than five."

Dathan shrugged. "Suit yourself. Just don't slow us down." He slammed a palm on the big metal door to the stairwell and it burst open, then he descended the stairs. "First place I'd like to patrol is our suite."

Yep, something was definitely up. Natasha's room was the safest place in the building and no cameras. If he wanted Zack and me with him there, then he wanted to talk without anyone else interfering. He probably hadn't anticipated my parents and Renzo tagging along.

We were on patrol after all, so we took our time and looked for signs of anything out of the norm. Finally, we arrived at the suite, gained access and filed in. Dathan made a show of checking every nook and cranny of the room before finally commanding our attention. "And now that we're all alone, listen up."

Renzo groaned. "Figured something seemed fishy. So why did you lure Zack and Autumn on your fake errand?"

"Actually, I predicted that the rest of you would demand to come along. Which is exactly what I wanted." Dathan's mouth quirked on one side.

My mom winced and then her head knocked against the wall. "Okay, Dathan, we give in. Why did you want us with you on this little adventure?"

"Because I'm afraid your queen might be too soft when it comes to her own," Dathan answered as he claimed a spot on the couch. "And I need all of you to back me up."

"Wait..." My dad hurled a warning glare at Dathan. "We're supposed to ignore our queen in your favor?"

"Absolutely." Dathan crossed an ankle over his knee. "Because you want to survive this. Sean and the other fifteen vanished from our radar for over an hour. We have no idea if during that time they were all actually sleeping or Ulric glamoured them, then wiped their memories. See, Sean's too smart to allow all his men to sleep without at least several staying awake to keep watch. Which means Her Majesty should've been able to reach someone during that hour. If Sean or anyone else was tampered with, we need to take precautions. Which Natasha apparently isn't inclined to do."

"I think you're underestimating her. Just because she's slow to admit you're right doesn't mean she'll ignore obvious dangers," my dad said.

"If Ulric had already gotten what he needed from someone else, it's possible that Sean's mind wasn't altered," Zack said hopefully.

"Then we still have the mystery of them not answering us." Dathan threaded his hands through his hair. "Besides, if Ulric already has all the info he needs, that's just as bad."

Renzo growled. "As much as I hate to admit it, Dathan is right and any of the crew could work against us."

"While I believe our queen is a shrewd leader, I'm also aware that her great affection for her people could be her downfall," my dad mumbled, squeezing his eyes shut for a moment. "Knowing her, she'd readily sacrifice herself to save them."

A hard edge glinted in Dathan's eyes. "Exactly. Regardless of the crew's best intentions, any of them could betray us all simply because Ulric gave them no choice."

"I agree," my mom said, arching into my dad like she was trying to comfort him. "Do you have a plan?"

"Not yet," Dathan said. "My first priority was to have this discussion where we wouldn't be heard. I don't have any other ideas at the moment except to keep an eye on the scouting crew. Might want to also watch over the other four who arrived late. We can't have any of them unwillingly follow Ulric's orders and make it impossible for us to win this."

How would Ulric affect Zack and me, since we were hybrids who'd had vampire blood? Also, my parents were ancient and Zack was part vampire. We might be safe... but what about the others? And while we were hiding in our room, we weren't there to help our own people.

"Anything could be happening up there." My stomach knotted. "Shouldn't we get back?"

"Yes." My mom glanced toward the door. "We need to return to the others."

"It's only been a few minutes, but yes." Dathan exhaled and he rose from the sofa when Zack and I made a beeline for the door. "Wait. I want to know where each of you are at all times. If you don't check in often enough, I'll come searching for you. Got it? We should do that patrol before we go back. We'll make it quick."

When we reentered the training area after a brief sweep of the building, Dathan's gaze immediately found Natasha. He grinned. "What did we miss?"

Natasha paused from swiping her sword against an imaginary enemy. "The scouting crew finished breakfast then went straight to their chambers to catch up on rest. I imagine they'll be there for several hours."

Dathan stared at his shoes, like the wheels in his head were turning. "I'm going to take a break and make some calls, check in with Cedric. Zack and Autumn can train with you guys while I'm gone." *I'll be patrolling the building again*, Dathan sent into my head. I assumed he shared that with my parents, Renzo and Zack too.

"I'll be in my suite catching up on work." Natasha laid her sword on the table. "I've gotten so behind on everything."

"I thought we were all going to travel in groups," I said.

"Everyone except me. I'll escort Natasha to her room. She'll be safe there." Dathan motioned for Natasha to follow as he headed out. After they disappeared, we resumed training.

Hours passed and neither of them returned. Dathan checked in telepathically every now and then, usually when I least expected it—like when my mom was coming at me with a weapon. Always good to know he was still alive but his random telepathic chats distracted me.

At five, we broke for dinner and crowded around the dining room table. Dathan took a break from patrolling and joined us. "Natasha is still busy in her suite. She's staying in for dinner."

We hadn't seen her since shortly after breakfast. I hoped she wasn't regretting joining us against Ulric.

"But she's okay?" Renzo asked.

"I talked to her before dinner," my dad said,

opening for another bite of casserole. "She's a little spooked, thinks Ulric is right under our nose and that's why the search party hasn't found him. Other than that, she's fine."

"She's got this place to run," my mom added, waving a finger to encompass the room. "A queen can only put off pressing matters for so long."

The rest of the meal was eaten in silence, each one of us lost in our own thoughts. Probably wondering where Ulric was hiding and when he'd strike. Geez, he was like a ghost. The monitors hadn't picked up anything, no alarms had gone off, and no sightings from the scouting crew or his men. Not since Yvonne had shown us the picture of him.

Where the hell was he? Yet somehow I could almost feel Ulric. Or maybe the tingling on the back of my neck was caused from paranoia and stress.

As I swallowed the last bite of peas, I froze. Where was Ivan who was usually cleaning up the table by now? I cocked my head to listen for the usual sounds. No pans clanging in the kitchen on the other side of the wall. No voices from other floors. No footfalls as people traveled from room to room. Nothing. "Hey, guys? It's a little too quiet, don't you think?"

Renzo slowly set down the glass of water he'd been about to sip from. "Has anyone checked in with Havers to make sure he's still monitoring the perimeters?"

"Havers," Dathan said aloud. "What's the current status?"

We waited for Havers to report in. I extended my hearing to other parts of the building... Nothing. Nothing at all.

"Where is everyone?" Zack glanced around, then cautiously ascended from his chair. After a moment, he zoomed to the doorway of our private dining area. He halted, listened for an instant, and then he was gone.

"Damn it, Zack." Renzo bolted out of the room after him.

They returned seconds later, both hovering close by while not exposing their backs to the open wall. "Not a soul around. Not on this floor anyway."

"Ah, hell." My dad pushed off his chair, reaching for my mom's hand. My heart pounded.

"Havers responded. He insists that the cameras are in good working order." Dathan slowly pivoted in his chair, taking in the every corner of the area.

My mom stiffened, on alert. "Considering the silence, I doubt that's the case. There's no way they could all vanish without someone being inside and Havers spotting something."

"Oh, no." My dad's face fell. "Natasha."

Dathan grasped my dad's arm before he could move. "Talk to her first. If she's still in her suite, get her to stay there. That's the safest place for her to be."

My mom muttered a curse. "Natasha answered. I strongly suggested she stay put."

"As did I." My dad scowled. "She'll stay. I hope."

"If she listens, it's temporary." Dathan peered out the door and surveyed the edges of the room. "Natasha is too noble and, as we already know, that's her flaw. Not to sound repetitive, but Ulric and his men will attack soon, so it's important we stay togeth—"

Glass shattered from the skylight above, followed by a whirring noise. I jumped out of the way just as a headless body crashed into the table.

CHAPTER SEVENTEEN
—— *Autumn* ——

SHARDS OF GLASS sprayed through the air. Food and plates shattered to the floor. By the smell, the headless body used to be a shape-shifter. But without a head, I had no idea who. A quick glance above revealed that someone had previously opened the hatch, leaving glass as the only barrier for intruders.

I backed up as a woman dropped from the broken skylight and landed on her feet. She offered us a smug look and then three more werewolves joined, dropping with a thud. Dathan vaulted and latched onto a rafter above. While he battled another werewolf trying to get through, he somehow clung to the ceiling and struck at anyone who got near the opening. *You guys are on your own until I get this thing shut.*

The four werewolves sneered and stepped toward us. Obviously, they didn't feel at a disadvantage, even being outnumbered with my parents, Renzo, Zack and me. Renzo brandished a dagger and I reached into my waistband for a throwing knife.

My dad swung an arm, shielding me and impelling me backward. Using his free hand, he whipped out a pistol with one of the biggest barrels I'd ever seen. "It won't kill you but it'll do some serious damage. Who wants it first?"

My eyes searched for Zack. *Where did you go?*

Getting weapons. He reappeared a split second later holding a huge rifle. "This won't kill you either. But I know from personal experience it'll knock you out for an hour or so."

"Tranquilizers?" The she-wolf threw her head back and laughed. "We're too strong for that now. None of you can stop us."

"Bring it on." A muscular guy in a tank top winked at me. "Don't worry, honey, I'll save you for last."

I shuddered and took another step back. My mom emitted a low guttural sound, moving in front of me. Between my mom and dad both shielding me, way to point out the weak link.

Keeping their bodies at an angle, alert and ready, the werewolves inched forward. My mom dipped down, her gaze trained on the newcomers, as she retrieved a dagger from her boot.

"Now!" my dad shouted.

I aimed a knife and it stuck in the muscular guy's shoulder. He flinched, his eyes flaring, and I threw another one that landed in his side. He gritted his teeth, yanked on the blade and pulled his arm back to throw it at me. Before he got a chance, I morphed into a bear, my jaws going straight for his arm holding the weapon.

He snarled and brandished another dagger, plunging it into my abdomen. Fire burned through me as I tore off his wrist, leaving a bloody stub. He howled and I went for his neck. I had no plans of letting this guy go. At least with him out of the fight, my parents and Renzo could handle the other three.

Shots fired, followed by shouts. I couldn't see what was happening behind me; I only knew I had to slow this guy down, no matter what. Then his movements became sluggish and I peered up. A dart protruded from his neck. I released him and he stumbled back.

Zack flashed me a grin and closed the distance.

As if the werewolf's body had already metabolized the tranquilizer, he straightened his spine and raised the bloody dagger he'd sank into my belly. "You have no idea what you're dealing with."

Zack shoved me out of the way, but I doubled back. The werewolf stalled mid-lunge, grunted, then his eyes rolled back. My dad came easily into view when the werewolf toppled to the floor. "Step aside and let us take care of this."

Yeah, right. If I stood around doing nothing, and we all died, it would be my own damn fault. But my dad was gone before I could argue. I glanced over to Zack who was already redirecting the huge rifle at the werewolf fighting my mother. But they were too fast for Zack to get a bead on the guy.

My mom's dagger lay a few feet away. *I'll help her. You get that guy who's all over Renzo.* I raced to the dagger, seized it and sank it into the werewolf's ribs hoping to hit his heart. He went limp and my mom knocked him away.

A head flew toward me and I veered to the side but the blood-soaked hair fanned out and brushed my arm as it passed. A shudder escaped me.

The she-wolf charged my dad, and my mom and Renzo lunged at her. She spun, gained purchase and sped off. I threw a knife and the blade landed in her back but it didn't slow her down. My mom and dad took off after her.

The air whirred once again and Dathan landed in front of us.

Renzo sent him a dark look. "Thanks for your help getting rid of the amped up werewolves."

"Four of them to five of you." Dathan's nostrils flared. "There's an emergency hatch up there which I closed over the broken skylight. Or else Ulric's men would've become an even bigger problem."

I grimaced. "Not like your petty bickering isn't important but, you know, we're at war. We're supposed to be sticking together. Shouldn't we be helping my parents catch that werewolf?"

"I'll find Olivia and Quentin. You guys figure out why Havers didn't alert us to the intruders. He's in there." Dathan jabbed a thumb toward a door all the way on the other side of the training area marked Security, then he vanished in a blur.

Zack and I raced to the security door with Renzo directly behind us. Renzo pounded a fist against the metal door. "Havers. Open up." After a moment of silence, he snarled. "No one is monitoring the damn cameras."

Mom, you guys okay? I asked them. *Did you catch that woman?*

We're fine, sweetheart. And, yes, we got her, she answered. *We're on our way back.* True to her word, they returned moments later with the woman draped across my dad's shoulders, Dathan right behind them. My dad let her slide off and her head thumped against the solid floor.

"Paralyzed?" Zack asked.

"I merely repositioned the knife Autumn had put in her back." My mom sidestepped when Zack approached. Always keeping a safe distance from him and Renzo. "Nice shot, by the way."

"People, we don't have time for ego stroking. We should already be cutting off their heads so they don't wake up." Renzo grabbed the paralyzed girl by the hair, made a clean slice across her neck, then let the head drop to the floor and roll away.

I squashed the urge to gag, certain that I'd never get used to beheading. Unfortunately, there was probably more of that to come.

"If Havers is under Ulric's control, he might've already opened all the other hatches. Let's move!" Renzo bellowed.

Dathan dragged the woman's body out of our path then sprinted to the security door. "Unless Ulric is already inside. In that case, he'll want the hatches to stay closed in case we call for reinforcements."

My chest felt weighted. "We should let Natasha know we're all okay so she doesn't come out," I said, hoping she would be smart and stay in her secure suite.

"Already done," my dad answered.

Dathan hammered on Havers's door. "Damn it, Havers. Let us in."

"We're not getting through that steel." My dad laid his ear against the door. "Someone is definitely in there."

"All of us together might be able to eventually break it," I said.

"We can't destroy the door because when we leave, the area must be secure so Ulric or his men can't access the room." Dathan rubbed his chin as he stared at the door.

"Someone around here knows how to get in that room or how to override the security. We need to locate everyone anyway, and get them all in one place," Zack said.

My dad glared at the panel beside the door. "Natasha, what's the code to get into the security room?"

While my mom kept watch to make sure no one snuck up behind us, my dad punched in the access code. When the door swung open, Havers jumped back and clutched his arms around his waist.

"Olivia, Quentin, guard the door," Dathan barked, advancing on Havers. "Why have you been telling everyone that the monitors weren't picking up anything? And why wouldn't you answer the door and let us in?"

Monitors filled the room, but the screens were filled with black and white static. Someone had disabled all the cameras outside. Anything could be happening out there. I checked over my shoulder to keep tabs on the entrance, but my dad and mom had it covered.

"I don't know." Havers's eyes widened, his gaze bouncing around the room, and then he slumped back onto a chair. "I'm doing things I don't want to do and I can't stop. And when I want to do something, I can't." He was shivering now, cowering from Dathan.

Renzo rounded on Havers. "Other than this room, where else have you been today?"

Havers whimpered. "I can't remember."

"Do you know where everyone went?" Zack asked Havers.

"Yes." Havers opened his mouth then blinked.

Dathan's words erupted in a raspy voice. "Tell us."

Havers whined, shrinking lower into the chair.

Renzo slammed his fist on the table. "Dathan, how do you dehypnotize someone?"

"That's the least of our worries," my dad said. "If Havers hasn't been out of the compound so Ulric could glamour him, that means Ulric is inside."

"Havers, are you able to tell us if you opened any of the hatches?" my mom asked.

"Uh..." Havers's eyes glazed over for an instant. When he snapped out of it, he used the back of his hand to wipe sweat off his forehead. "I can tell you that none of the hatches are open at the moment."

"How do we know he wasn't programmed to say that?" Renzo growled, checking the controls and studying the readouts. "He could've opened the hatches earlier."

"Obviously, Havers wouldn't do that of his own volition. Go easy on him," my dad said. "I'd love to know how long he's been under Ulric's control."

"Must've been recently." I chewed my bottom lip. "Otherwise Ulric would've attacked when he first got here, taken us by surprise. Or while the scouting crew was gone and he had less people to fight."

"I think you're right." Renzo ground his teeth. "Without control over the monitors, Ulric couldn't get the rest of his crew inside."

"Havers, where is Ulric?" Dathan asked.

Havers held the sides of his head, squeezing his eyes shut.

"He can't answer." Renzo's fists clenched. "How do we get him back under his own control?"

"Ulric is the only one who can undo it," Dathan hissed. "If not willingly, then by his own death."

"Then let's go kill him." A vein pulsed at Zack's neck.

"Patience, Zack." Dathan turned to my dad. "Have you checked in with Natasha to make sure she's okay?"

"I did a couple minutes ago. She's not answering." My dad's brows furrowed. "I also tried Sean, Yvonne, Persius, Egon, Kieran, Haji... nothing."

"She's probably busy with something else." My stomach twisted and I hoped that was the explanation for the lack of response. "Maybe you'll hear from her soon."

But it wasn't like Natasha not to answer. And while she was out there, possibly hurt or dead, we were safe. Although I was grateful to be alive and not in a confrontation with Ulric—yet—guilt pricked at my conscience for dragging Natasha and her people into our fight.

"Havers, is there anything you can think of that you're able to tell us?" I asked, searching for a loophole in the glamour. "Can you tell us when you stopped being able to answer our questions?"

Havers leaped up from his chair. "It was a couple hours ago."

"Where is Ulric?" my mom demanded.

Havers's mouth fell open as if he wanted words to come out, but instead he squeaked and dropped down to his chair.

My dad loomed over Havers and glared. "Is there anything you can tell us that will help us save *your* life?"

"Dad, it's not his fault." I knelt in front of Havers. "Are you expecting anyone to come back for you?"

Havers stared at his shoes.

I patted Havers on the knee, then stood. "Mom, Dad, we can beat Ulric. I'm sure of it."

"Ulric won't be alone, sweetheart. Even if he is, we can't stay here while he's figuring out how to let in more werewolves. For all we know he'll have us battling our own people." My mom shook her head. "We need to find him before he does any more damage."

"Agreed," my dad said. "Unfortunately, Ulric's been one step ahead of us this whole time."

Renzo's hands fisted. "Between our own people who could be fighting on Ulric's behalf, and anyone else he may have let inside, we could be screwed."

Dathan's jaw flexed. "That's assuming our crew is still alive."

I didn't want them hypnotized into coming after us and I didn't want to have to fight them. But I didn't want them dead either. The back of my neck prickled. This was so much worse than I'd imagined when I'd first noticed the silence. I'd been naïve to ever believe we had any advantage over Ulric.

Dathan patted himself for the dagger in his waistband as he moved to the door. "I'm better equipped to deal with Ulric. Which two of you are coming with me?"

"We agreed to stay together, remember?" I asked, not wanting any of them where I couldn't help protect them. And vice versa.

"Someone needs to stay here, make sure Havers doesn't do anything to make things worse, like open the hatches and let more of Ulric's men inside." My mom's jaw clenched. "We have to split up."

Crap, I didn't care for that prospect at all. "And what if while you're out looking for Ulric, he ends up here?"

"Then you contact me telepathically." Dathan redirected to my dad. "Are you coming or staying?"

"I'm not leaving you to deal with that psycho on your own." My dad checked his weapons.

"I'll go with you," my mom volunteered, glancing my way.

Dathan wagged a finger at Zack and Renzo. "You two should stay here with Autumn. This room controls every door and camera in the building and must be kept secure. Let's not underestimate Ulric."

No matter who stayed, someone I loved would be gone and any of them could be hurt or killed. But my parents were ancient and stood a better chance against Ulric than Renzo or Zack. I nodded numbly, trying not to think about what could happen to anyone who came face-to-face with Ulric.

I hurled myself at mom, then pulled my dad into the hug. "Be safe."

They folded their arms around me, nearly crushing my ribs. "We'll be back soon."

They couldn't guarantee that, but I had to hope. After the door locked behind them, all I could do was wait...

CHAPTER EIGHTEEN
———— *Autumn* ————

THE DE LUCA men and I were confined to one room while Dathan and my parents went out and did the dirty work. I hated feeling as useless as the guy we were guarding.

But what if the security room and equipment didn't need to be guarded? Maybe Havers could be useful again if I found a loophole in Ulric's compulsion. I just had to ask the right questions.

"Havers, is there a way to seal this room so we could leave without anyone but us getting in? If we're not tied to this area, we can be finding the guy who did this to you."

Havers's eyes brightened. "Yes."

A few minutes later, Havers showed us how to change the passwords, which we relayed telepathically to Dathan. Since we couldn't trust Havers, we kept the information to ourselves. We scanned the vicinity as we crept out of the security room and into the training area.

"Dathan just checked in. They're about to inspect the park and garage below," Renzo said, nabbing more weapons.

Zack handed me four more daggers. "Havers, can we secure the rest of the place like we did with your area, so no one can compromise that section again?"

"Yes. We have an emergency feature installed on every door." Havers steered us into the hallway. "After we make sure no one's there, we'll leave and seal it."

"Other than the security room, is there a master control anywhere else?" I asked, readjusting the extra daggers in my waistband.

"We always have a fail-safe which can override the system, in case something like this happens," Havers said. "It's in the parking structure."

That was where Renzo said Dathan and my parents were headed, which would be the most convenient place for them to be, since it would be the last place we would secure. Except that was most likely where Ulric was waiting for us. As empty as this place was, I was betting he had the rest of the shape-shifters with him—also under his control.

My parents were out there somewhere. Letting them go was a huge mistake. *Mom?*

After several moments of silence, I gulped as my breathing quickened and my blood roared in my ears. This sucked. "My mom's not answering."

"We'd better hurry. But even if we seal each door as we go, we'll likely always have that unknown access open wherever Ulric got in," Renzo muttered, punching in a code. A sheet of metal slid over, sealing it shut and covering the doorknob.

"Havers, as head of security you're the expert on

everything about this place, right?" Zack asked as we moved in unison down the corridor. "If there's a way to get in that you don't know about, the opening was probably created by Ulric, correct?"

"Correct. But this place is built of titanium, big solid thick pieces of it." Havers lead the way to the stairwell. "Even if someone managed to burrow through it using superhuman strength, it would take a while. I imagine we'd hear the scraping against the shell or feel the vibrations."

We reached the stairs and Zack raised one brow. "There are a lot of windows and skylights. If Ulric got in through any of them, you would've seen and alerted someone since you wouldn't have been under Ulric's control without him making some kind of contact with you first. Which means Ulric got through to someone else who then lured you to wherever Ulric was. And that's when he hypnotized you, right?"

When Havers's mouth opened and his eyes glazed over, I gritted my teeth. Zack nudged Havers, jolting him out of his stupor, and we descended the stairs.

I rushed the last of the steps and passed everyone. At the landing, the scent of unfamiliar wolf smothered me. My heart pounded against my ribs as I held my arms out and blocked the door. *Ulric is down here. Dathan and my parents are probably in trouble. Before we barge in there, we'd better have a plan.*

Three of us against Ulric and everyone else? The plan better be brilliant. Renzo's jaw tensed as he glared at the door. *Because there's no way Ulric didn't hear us coming down the stairs. Did you try Dathan?*

Not yet. I'd been so consumed with worry over my parents that I'd momentarily forgotten Dathan had been with them. *Dathan, where are you?*

In the garage near the stairwell. Your parents and I split up to cover more ground. I was about to venture into the garage in search of them, but they're not answering.

You left them? Are you crazy?

For a matter of seconds. And when I exited the park, I caught the stench and knew something was wrong. Where are you?

We're right next to you on the other side of the door. I hesitated, wondering if it was safe to open it. But Dathan would've warned me. I unlocked the door and pulled it open, Dathan slid through, then shut the door and locked it.

If Ulric already knows we're here, what are we waiting for? Unless there's another way to get inside, Zack said. *Havers?*

We already sealed the other doors, Havers answered. *This is the only way in.*

He'll know we're coming no matter how we get there. We have no choice but to go in and face him, I said. The sooner I got to my parents, the better.

Energy swirled between Dathan and Zack but before I could ask them what was up, Dathan rounded on me and lifted my chin with an index finger. "Ulric won't hurt your parents yet because he needs them alive to manipulate us. Keep your cool."

I nodded, although the wrenching in my gut

screamed at me to stop wasting time. "I will. But we need to get going."

"The garage is thick with scents of werewolf and shape-shifter." Dathan positioned himself in front of the door so I couldn't push past him. "I know you, Autumn. You don't want to kill shape-shifters who've been glamoured into fighting us. Anyone you don't recognize is likely one of Ulric's men. Kill them. Everyone else, just try to temporarily incapacitate them."

"That's going to burn time," Renzo growled. "But we don't have a choice."

"We have extra knives on hand to paralyze them." I glanced between Dathan and Renzo. "If for some reason I can't quickly get to their heart, any advice on the most efficient way to neutralize someone without killing them?"

"Cut off their limbs, break their necks—anything that forces them to heal and takes them out of the game." Dathan nodded once, then stepped aside.

I gripped the handle and shoved the door open. Dathan slipped in front of me and led the way. We crept through the dark structure, keeping our noses in the air for any shifts in scents, our ears alert for any movement.

The sound of footfall on dirt and rustling fabric reached us and the next instant, we were surrounded. Dathan spun, watching our backs and we formed a circle around Havers. A quick assessment told me Dathan was right—Ulric had gotten to our entire army. And now we'd have to fight the ones he hadn't already killed. Adrenaline roared through my limbs, making them tremble.

"Give up now and come quietly, and we won't have to hurt you." Egon raised his sword and tipped the edge toward Zack.

There's only ten of them. We can handle this, Renzo said, his back bumping mine. *And when I say we, I really mean Dathan.*

Dathan chuckled into our heads. *You just make sure nothing happens to Zack or Autumn. One...*

Oh, hell. This was it. I slowly reached for a dagger, reminding myself that I was more powerful than Egon or any of these shifters. I just had to stay focused.

Two...

I let the life essence of each one of them seep into me, become one with mine. Without looking, I knew where each one stood. I knew that Egon was perspiring and the shape-shifter to my right struggled to keep his heart from hammering out of his chest.

Three.

I ducked as Egon sliced his sword through the air then I sank my dagger into his heart. As he plunged backward, his arm flailed and I grabbed the sword from his hand, twisted and cut it through the air to land in a shape-shifter lunging toward me. It penetrated his heart, paralyzing him.

Dathan had already taken down three guys and they lay on the dirt, blood oozing from an open wound. Renzo was fighting two shifters and Havers was trying to get a bead on one of them. "Havers!" I grabbed one of the knives from my waistband and tossed it to him.

I flinched when I spotted Zack feeding on a shape-shifter. What the hell? Zack dropped the guy, then circled around to find another opponent. But we were the only ones left standing.

Dathan wiped his mouth and grinned. "Been a while since I had warm blood straight from the vein."

Zack had the same, apparently. I stared at him, my eyes practically bulging out of their sockets. "W-was that more efficient?"

"I just learned how to glamour... which can only be done when feeding. Better than hurting them." Zack shrugged. "So, yeah, looks like I'll be well fed by the time we're done."

I swallowed, my breath unsteady. This was not something I wanted to think about right now. "Okay. Let's move on."

Renzo forged ahead through the parking structure and the rest of us followed.

"Although werewolves are kind of bitter." Zack's eyes ping-ponged from me to our surroundings.

He was doing what he had to do, but I had an inkling that it bothered him. I glanced away to pay attention to where we were going, my gaze circling the structure for any movement.

"Ew. Too much information, Zack," Havers said, staying close to Dathan.

"They'll be more clever next time," Dathan said.

"Maybe even try to pick us off one by one."

"Then we'll stick together." Renzo halted. Ahead of him was a line of around twenty shape-shifters. Our former army, including Sean, Yvonne, Kieran and Haji.

I slowed my breathing, getting a read on each of them—Haji shifting his weight, the rapid heartbeat of the shape-shifter closest to me, a female werewolf zeroing in on Havers, Yvonne's fingers twitching around a dagger, Sean holding his breath.

"I realize you all have no choice but to attack." Dathan inched forward, his fingers twitching. "We'll try not to kill you." *One... two... three.*

As I lunged at the female werewolf, I shifted into a bear midair. My jaws clamped onto her shoulder and I jerked my head side to side, nearly disconnecting her arm in seconds. She screamed, stabbing me with her free hand. I threw my weight on her, my fangs shredding her knife-wielding arm. Satisfied she was neutralized for a while, I rolled to avoid an incoming knife from behind and shifted back to my human form. The blade plunged into my hip. Sean. I shoved my palm into his nose and retrieved the knife from my waist, sinking it into his chest.

Two down. My hip already healing, I vaulted into the air, reaching for another knife from my waistband. I plunged it into the Haji's back just as he was about to stab Havers, then pivoted and jumped on Kieran as he struck at Renzo. Grabbing his head with both hands, I wrenched it around and he dropped.

"Sorry, Kieran." I leapt off him, my eyes searching

for my next opponent just as Renzo neutralized Yvonne. She collapsed to the floor, a handle sticking out of her chest.

I released all the air in my lungs seeing my team still standing.

A vertical index finger over Dathan's lip told us to be quiet. *It'll take Ulric a moment to figure out which side won that battle.* His gaze found mine. *Let's find your parents.*

An eerie quiet filled the large space, making the whole thing seem even creepier and scarier. I stole past the cars behind Dathan, peering between them in our hunt for Ulric, our necks straining to see all around. We neared the last row of cars in the corner, and the energy in the space changed, becoming thicker and charged. I froze.

"At last," the man said, drawing out the last two letters. "We've been waiting."

Dathan stepped around me and moved to my left, bright lights momentarily blinding me. My eyes adjusted and then the air stuck in my lungs.

The stranger, who had to be Ulric, was crouched against the wall holding a blade to my mom's throat. Except she had no throat. Crimson drenched the collar of her once baby-blue T-shirt and her head hung limply on her shoulder. An extra big splotch of crimson covered her abdomen and acid curled in my gut at the sheer amount of blood. My dad stood a few feet away, his arms hanging at his sides.

"One slip of the blade and she's gone." Ulric's eyes

glinted with a hint of insanity as he grinned at us. "Eli here is awfully glad you two could make it to the party."

Two? I glanced over my shoulder but there wasn't anything there other than walls, rows of cars and the beams above. To our right was the giant elevator we'd used to move the Navigator from the underground tunnel. The door was open. I didn't have to wonder how Ulric got in.

Where did Havers, Renzo and Zack go?

"I have to say, I've been monumentally impressed at your ability to evade me these centuries." He sent my dad an odd look that seemed a mixture of respect and loathing. "The last fifty years, I've been following so far behind, I wasn't sure if I was on the right trail. You've caused me a good deal of trouble. The sweeter the kill."

"How are you going to kill all four of us, Ulric?" Dathan asked, inching forward. "The rest of your men can't access the parking lot. It's just us."

"The rest of my men? Why would I need to bring my own army when I can borrow yours?" Ulric hummed and his eyes flicked to mine. "Egon has been so helpful, by the way."

Egon? I reminded myself that Egon hadn't meant to hurt anyone. He probably wasn't even aware of his actions.

My lids felt droopy, my mind fuzzy. Then that dissipated, replaced by an urge to attack Dathan that nearly consumed me. My hands fisted and I turned toward him.

I can feel him trying to control your mind. Don't let

him, Dathan said, his gaze riveted to Ulric. *You can block his thoughts. Focus.*

That son of a bitch! I pushed Ulric out of my head and closed myself off, grateful I'd had plenty of practice with mental gymnastics the last few months. I gripped one of the knives in my pocket and stepped into Ulric's line of vision. "Nice try," I growled. "It may have worked on whoever let you in. Won't work on me."

One side of Ulric's mouth skewed and his gaze wavered, making him seem less confident than a moment before.

"Despite your stolen powers, you're no match for me," Dathan said. "Even if you succeeded in finishing off Olivia, we'll attack. At least one of us will live and you'll be dead. Makes no sense."

Ulric seemed recovered from the surprise of not being able to compel me, snickering quietly. "If by some miracle you survive today, then you'll die tomorrow. Either way, I would've succeeded in doing what I came here for."

"And what's that?" Dathan asked, inching forward as soon as Ulric glanced at my mom.

"The death of Hannah and Eli. After centuries of pursuit, I've finally got them."

It's probably best Ulric not know I'm their daughter, I told Dathan.

Autumn, my dad snuck a peek at me, *you shouldn't be here. I couldn't bear it if anything happened to you too. Back up and run, find Zack, and go.*

How would I go on if something happened to you? Could I live with myself after leaving my parents to die and doing nothing at all to help? *I'm not leaving.*

Ulric studied me and the blade slacked at my mother's neck. "You have an uncanny resemblance to her."

How could he be so casual as my mom lay there in his arms barely alive? Fury filled me but I squashed it and lifted a careless shoulder. "So what? You resemble a douche bag teacher I had last year." Except Mr. Olander's hair was never greasy. Ulric's dark blond stringy hair clung to his neck and shoulders like it hadn't been washed or brushed in days. He hadn't shaved in forever.

"You need to show respect for your elders," Ulric rasped.

"Yeah?" I asked, as my scalp prickled. I mentally pushed Ulric out. "And if I don't, what are you going to do about it? Will you choke me to death with your filthy hands? I guess it's hard to find time to bathe when you're too busy killing innocent people."

Dathan snorted. *If nothing else, you're lessening his triumph.*

Ulric's face flushed. "You dare to speak to me that way. I could tear her head off in one instant and kill you in the next."

"I doubt you'd make it past us. And she means nothing to me so I have nothing to lose," I bluffed, taking a step forward, and stealthily stuffing my hands in my back pocket. "Can we speed this up so you'll be one step closer to being dead?"

"You underestimate me," Ulric hissed. "Do you think I'd begin battle with her as my only leverage?"

"What's your other leverage?" Dathan asked.

Ulric sneered. "This place is going to blow up, and I'm the only one who knows when and how. If I die, the bomb goes off and no one can stop it. If I live, then I detonate it after I get out."

I rolled my eyes and edged closer to him. "If I had a dollar for every time someone's threatened to kill me."

In my peripheral, Dathan stood beside my dad. I could feel the energy radiating off Dathan, and I wondered what he was saying. *Keep distracting Ulric, little one, he told me. Quentin and I will take care of the rest.*

Let us handle this, sweetheart, my dad added.

I couldn't blame my dad for wanting to keep me from dying, if possible. But I'd already resigned myself to being incapable of staying on the sidelines. "If I had a nickel for every time someone *thought* they could kill me."

Ulric pinned me with a stare. "You have no idea what you're dealing with."

"Actually, I do." I gripped the throwing knives in my back pocket, and faced Dathan. "Shall we tell him?"

"Tell me what? That you have no plan, except to begin preparations for your funerals?" Ulric chuckled.

Autumn, we're coming in, Zack told me. *On the count of five, distract him. One...*

I'd *already* been distracting Ulric. My mind raced but I couldn't think of a damn thing to say. Well, there was one thing I could *do.*

Two...

As Dathan glanced between Ulric and me, I started to turn back to Ulric. What I was about to do was risky. And I could hurt my mom. But it would distract Ulric and my mom would heal.

Three...

"You're stalling," Ulric said, a smug look on his face. "Nothing you do will change the outcome. But I'm happy to watch you try."

"Or maybe we're stalling because we love your company." While my right arm was still out of his line of vision, I pulled out a knife, readied it.

Four...

As I finished turning back to face him, I threw the blade and nailed Ulric in the neck. His grip on my mother loosened and a blaze ignited in his eyes.

Five...

Zack burst into our corner. When Ulric reached up to remove the knife I'd sunk into his neck, my dad leaped on him. Dathan jumped in and they tackled Ulric. I caught my mom before her head slammed against the ground and I dragged her away.

Renzo pressed a huge barrel to Ulric's head. "It won't kill you but it will do a lot of damage. And while your brains are scrambled, we'll finish you off."

"Wait." My dad's palm flew up. "There's a bomb somewhere and only he knows where it is."

"Where's the bomb, Ulric?" Dathan demanded as he used Ulric's sword against him. "Don't make me torture it out of you."

Ulric clucked his tongue and squeaked out a laugh. "You can't kill me or you'll never find Natasha."

Ulric had Natasha? He'd covered all his bases to ensure we didn't kill him. I glanced up at my dad. His face had gone gray and his grip loosened on the sword. "Don't do it yet," I said.

"Where is Natasha?" Dathan demanded.

"And lose my leverage?" Ulric's mouth crooked.

Dathan removed the sword and stepped back. "Unfortunately, he's right. As much as I'd love to end him right now, we can't. We also have to get out of here without exploding."

"Natasha's alive. She answered." My dad's eyes darkened. "She's been taken to King Mortimer."

My breath caught. Centuries ago Mortimer had kept Natasha prisoner as a rat for years and she'd finally escaped—only to come full circle.

"Mortimer will use her as bait in case Ulric fails. If he succeeds in killing you both, Natasha dies." Dathan knelt next to my mom and bit his wrist to open a vein, then let his blood drip onto her neck. "This will help a little with the healing process."

"Where's the bomb?" Renzo butted the gun against Ulric's head.

"That bomb is my insurance that I'll live through this." Ulric flashed us a maniacal grin. "And if any of you make a stupid move, you have less than two minutes to get out of the building. When my heart stops, the timer starts."

The detonator was in Ulric's chest? Disgusting.

And in order for us to get control of the detonator, he'd probably have to die. Either way, we couldn't stop the bomb from going off.

"I know where the bomb is," Havers told us.

I'd been so wrapped up in Ulric that I hadn't noticed Havers come in with Zack and Renzo. "Where is it?" I asked.

All eyes went to Havers and his eyes clouded over. "Uh… I can't say."

"It's true." Ulric snickered. "He can't say."

"Then we have only one option." My dad swung his sword and it came crashing down. Ulric's head split down the middle.

I sprung back, swallowing the urge to gag. Gross. "Geez, Dad."

He sliced the sword again, this time horizontal and pieces of Ulric's skull sprayed. Blood splattered and chunks of long stringy hair soared through the air. I averted my gaze although Zack had already stepped in front of me to block the image.

One more swipe of the blade removed any part of Ulric's head from his neck and the rest of him toppled over.

"Now that he's dead, can you tell us, Havers?" my dad asked. "And tell us quickly because according to Ulric, we have two minutes."

"Yeah. But you're not going to like it." Havers gulped, then spiraled to face Dathan. Energy swirled between them.

Adrenaline roared through my limbs as I waited

with dread. Energy swirled around me so someone was telling someone something. I wanted in on it. "We've got less than two minutes. Where's the bomb?"

Dathan shoved my dad aside and thrust his fist into my mother's abdomen. She yelped and her eyes fluttered. When he withdrew his fist, he held several sticks that had to be explosives. The bomb had been inside her the whole time? That explained all the blood I'd seen earlier on her stomach. Revulsion blanketed me and I swayed.

"Run for cover!" Dathan yelled then disappeared in a whoosh, taking the bomb with him. My mom moaned and my dad dropped the sword to scoop her up into his arms.

"We've got less than a minute. This way," my dad said, jerking his head toward the elevator shaft, the opposite direction Dathan had gone.

"What about everyone we paralyzed? They can't move. Zack, undo your glamour on the ones you took out." I raced across the parking lot to the group we'd fought earlier. As I passed each one—Egon, Sean, Kieran and a few others—I swooped, plucking knives out of their chests. Some were already snapping out of their hypnotic state. "This place is going to blow in a matter of seconds. Run for cover! Take them with you," I said, pointing at the ones who lay unconscious for other reasons than a stake through the heart.

They got busy, rescuing their own and I booked it to the elevator, charging toward the thick metal door. It slammed shut, grazing my heel, and I landed at the far corner of the shaft next to my mom and Zack.

Renzo threw himself over Zack and me, shielding us as thunder rolled into a deafening boom and amplified beyond. The narrow cracks of the metal walls of what might serve as our coffin widened into chasms, white powder and adobe from above showering down.

High above, a loose beam plummeted. Renzo pressed into us, flattening us against the ground. Dust fell around us and the trembling floor beneath our bellies groaned. As metal scraped against metal, I knew the explosion hadn't finished destroying the place. Titanium reinforced or not, obviously no metal was indestructible.

Renzo grunted when a chunk of rock slammed into his shoulder, then more slabs of granite and rock rained down until all I could do was crouch and wait.

And then silence.

Zack wiggled beside me. *Are you okay?*

I lay face down, with too much weight on me to move. And I was pretty sure something had sliced through me. *I still have my head. You?*

Probably just bruised. Very big bruises. But I'll live.

Good. Dad? Mom?

She's alive, my dad replied. *And I'll be okay in a few minutes.*

I flinched, hoping Dathan had gotten far enough away from the explosion. He had to be alive. He had to. *Hey, are you okay?* After a beat, I tried again. *Dathan, answer me.*

Feeling my body heal and regain strength, I placed my palms under my chest and pushed up. Renzo slid off me, along with the chunks of the building. White powder wafted into the air with each move. I crawled over to where my dad was emerging from a pile of debris. I helped him remove the wires and metal pieces that had buried my mom and in a matter of seconds, we'd uncovered her. I frantically examined the length of her for more injuries. Her head was connected and I whimpered in relief.

"She'll be okay," my dad said. "Eventually. Go help Renzo."

I circled around but he and Zack were already dusting themselves off. They staggered over the debris and limped toward us. I wrapped myself around Zack, lending him some support until he stabilized.

"I wish werewolf blood healed like vampire blood." Although Dathan dribbled some on my mom's neck just before the explosion, he hadn't let her feed from him. For some crazy reason, he'd shared his blood with Zack and me, but his generosity didn't extend to anyone else. My mom would have to heal the hard way. And that would take time.

But we needed her help to rescue Natasha. We needed Dathan too.

Dathan, I shouted into his head, wherever he was. *Are you okay?*

Not really, Dathan answered.

Fear coiled in my stomach at how far away he sounded. But at least he'd answered. For how much longer he'd be able to, I didn't know. *Where are you?*

I'm in the park. I'm not strong enough to dig myself out.

There's so much damage to the structure, I told him. *I wouldn't even know where to begin searching for you.*

When I ran with the bomb, I didn't have time to get away from it. Look for the part of the building with the most destruction and that's where I'll be.

How messed up was he? How much agony was he in? "Dathan's buried in the park and he needs our help."

"I'll have a look around, see if I can find a clear path to the park." Renzo slipped his hands under the elevator door and heaved it open. Thin pipes, wood chunks and wires tumbled into the elevator before he vanished. By the look on my dad's face as he stroked my mom's hair, he wasn't anxious to go anywhere. I was rather tired myself.

Renzo reappeared, nearly tripping on a thick wire. "The ceiling is caved in, which would require mining through half a block of this mess. Might be easier to get above ground, and then dig vertically."

"How about the rest of our guys?" I asked. "Did you see anyone?"

"No. We don't know how far they got so we wouldn't know where to start looking for them. Dathan is a bigger priority right now." Renzo pointed up. "Once we're outside, we can assess the damage."

"I'll help you with her," Zack told my dad.

My mom's eyes fluttered open. "I might be able to walk."

Relief flooded me at hearing her voice. She was going to be fine—if we got out of the building alive.

"Mom, no, we're climbing straight up. You need to save your strength for healing once we get out of here. Let them help."

My dad hoisted her up. I stepped toward the center, careful not to skid on the mound of rubble, and glanced above. The shaft had been compromised, for sure, but only a few pieces of wall were in our way. I could see a sliver of sky.

Renzo gripped a ledge above and lifted himself off the ground. "Once we get out of here, we have an awful lot of people to locate and rescue. With only us four, it's going to be slow and we'll be vulnerable the whole time."

We'd have to excavate every inch of the place to make sure we got everyone. And all that time, anyone still alive could be suffering. "Maybe the people at the nearby ranch can help," I said, finding my footing and following Renzo up the shaft.

"The ranch is maintained by humans who would ask too many questions, and we don't have a telepathic connection to any other shape-shifters around who may be willing to help." My dad huffed from the floor below as he took my mom's weight and began climbing. My mom clung to my dad's back, her arms trembling with effort as he climbed higher up the vertical passage.

Zack was just below with a good grip on her legs, taking some of the load off my dad. With Zack's support, she could expend less energy to hang on. Still, watching my mom struggle through the pain of her wounds didn't make me feel much better about the situation.

Her head bent forward against my dad's shoulder for support and her hair was matted with sweat and dried blood. I wanted to ask her if she was all right, but I could tell she wasn't. She'd lost too much blood and the damage too great. I didn't want to distract her and risk her letting go of my dad. I kept reminding myself that if she didn't have the strength to hold on and she fell back down the shaft, she'd live. She'd live and she'd heal.

Renzo reached the top and held out a hand for me. I took it and heaved myself to the other side. Dad was right behind me carrying my mom, and Zack behind them. When my dad was close enough, I reached for my mom's arm and Renzo grabbed under her shoulder. Together, we relieved my dad of my mother and gently laid her on a patch of grass. She sighed and closed her eyes. By her slack expression, I knew she had already passed out. I brushed a wisp of hair off her forehead, wishing I had a magic wand to heal her. I suppose it could be worse though. She could be human and already dead.

I rose to scan the area and froze. "You've gotta be kidding me."

Renzo's jaw set as he surveyed the mountain. "My thoughts exactly."

"It's as if nothing happened," Zack mumbled. "All that destruction below and the rest of the world slept through it."

"They're probably reporting an earthquake as we speak." In the distance, I spotted the ranch and just beyond that, the small town we'd driven through. None of those people had a clue that we had friends trapped below. Considering we couldn't have any of them discovering we were supernaturals—which they would if they found one of the crew horribly damaged yet somehow alive—we couldn't involve them.

Once we located Dathan, how many feet would we have to dig through to get to him? Where are you? I waited a beat. "Dathan's not answering."

"Let's call Cedric," Zack said. "He'll send help for his king."

CHAPTER NINETEEN
——— *Autumn* ———

AN HOUR OR so later, some of Cedric's most trusted people arrived by private jet—Kayla and Joseph, along with three others I'd met at the palace but hadn't gotten to know. After my dad had settled my mom under a tree over several layers of blankets—thankfully the vampires had brought supplies—my dad and Kayla jogged into town. They rented a backhoe and flood lights, then picked up food to help the injured with healing.

Zack and I spent every moment hunting for Dathan who hadn't replied since before we'd called the vampires for help. Because he was probably unconscious, the energy he emitted was nearly nil and the mounds of rubble covering him made the little trace of him even harder to detect. The bomb had annihilated access to the underground park. The area was so vast and Dathan was buried under who knew how many feet of earth. Flying blind could involve endless digging.

Renzo went back inside the compound through the elevator shaft in search of anyone still alive. Although he had navigated us closer to where the park might be, too many barriers blocked him from searching for others. Dathan was our priority anyway. But we couldn't locate him any time soon without his help.

Meanwhile, he could be dying or dead. Maybe he'd been nearly decapitated by the bomb and when he'd spoken silently to me, his head and nerves had finished detaching. And now he was gone...

I had to keep the faith. As much as Dathan irritated me, I couldn't deny how attached I'd grown to him. Not in a normal sense or any way that I'd ever experienced or could explain. But I cared deeply for him, that much I knew.

He was alive. He had to be.

My dad kept the backhoe running constantly, taking shifts with Zack while the rest of us used shovels. Every few hours, someone made food runs. I just wished my mom would heal faster.

"Mom, how are you holding up?" I asked, taking a quick break from the manual labor.

She sat up on her elbows. "Better. Not ready for battle yet, but I'll be able to get around on my own soon."

It would be sooner if she had vampire blood. We had vampires around now, but I couldn't ask any of them to share with my mom. Vampires were stingy that way, but I couldn't blame them.

I watched Zack shovel another load of rocks and drywall into a wheelbarrow. Wait... he was a hybrid, so he was part vampire. Would his blood have the same or similar effect as Dathan's? The sooner my mom healed, the sooner we could find Dathan and the rest of our people, then get the hell out of there and rescue my aunt.

Zack? Maybe your hybrid blood would help heal my mom. What do you think about giving it a shot?

He straightened, chucked a crumbling hunk of adobe into the wheelbarrow, and sped over to me. "It's worth a try."

I withdrew a throwing knife from my back pocket and passed it to Zack. He sliced his wrist and thrust it toward my mom. "I'm part vampire, remember? This might help. Drink up."

My mom grimaced before clamping onto his wrist and drinking. *It's working.* After a few moments, she nudged his wrist away. "Thank you."

My dad jogged over and gave him a man-nod. "Yes, thank you, Zack. Your color's better," he told my mom. "But considering the severity of your injuries, you still need to take it easy."

I didn't listen to my mom's reply as I scanned for Zack who'd vanished. I spotted him in the same place already back to work. I wanted Dathan found and freed as much as anyone else. But Zack could afford to waste a couple more seconds. I sprinted to him, climbed up onto the backhoe and threw my arms around him. *My mom hasn't exactly been gracious when it comes to you and your dad. And she may not come around for a long time.* Not while she was keeping her werewolfness under cover. *I appreciate you overlooking that.*

He kissed my forehead. *You're welcome. Now get a shovel.*

"I will if you refuel." I brushed away a tear with the back of my hand, then snagged the steering wheel and nudged him aside.

"Deal." He dropped a kiss on my cheek and slid off the seat.

Locating Dathan would be so much easier if he would answer and guide us. *Dathan, damn it, where are you?*

What time is it? Dathan's signal seemed a bit stronger.

It's the middle of the night. Why haven't you been answering? I've been trying to reach you for hours.

Due to the severity of my injuries, I required some sleep. My healing would accelerate if you would find me and feed me.

Right, one of us would likely have to supply him with blood. I'd do it in a heartbeat. *My blood is your blood. Now where the hell are you?*

I can't explain where I am because I'm buried and can't see. He paused a moment. *Except... you and Zack have shared my blood. You should be able to sense me.*

Yeah, I should. But I didn't. Why? Was he buried too deep and too far away? Or maybe I just needed to rely more on my supernatural perceptions.

I dropped to my knees to get closer to him, then shut my eyes and tuned out everything else as I crawled over the clumps of dirt and pieces of wood, expanding my mind to include Dathan.

"Autumn, what are you doing?"

I glanced up and offered Kayla a brief smile before returning to my quest. "Searching for Dathan."

As I crept along the ground I shut everything out but him. In the distance someone was talking but I stayed focused. I changed direction when my gut told me to, stayed on the path when the connection to Dathan grew stronger. My knees scraped a rock and I barely felt it. My palm met with something squishy and I kept going.

I stopped. *I found you.*

I knew you would, Dathan said.

Relief swept through me and I could almost feel his smile. It wasn't just because we would have his help and protection while rescuing my aunt. Even if I didn't want to be, and no matter how many times he acted like a douche, he was more good than bad. And he'd sacrificed himself so the rest of us wouldn't get blown up. I'd never forget that.

† † †

What seemed eons later, we'd dug to the deepest part of the structure, through tons of debris at the farthest corner of the underground park. As I got closer to Dathan and removed parts of the broken building, others were nearby to haul it away. We'd created a kind of canyon where we could easily climb in and out.

I balanced myself, my knees wedged against a big rock as I reached down to remove the rest of the chunks and gravel to expose Dathan's face. Dried blood crusted over mutilated skin and I was pretty sure the white over his cheekbone was actual bone. As if half of his face had been blown off.

The undamaged corner of his mouth curved up as he opened his eyes. "There you are, sugar," he said in a gravelly voice.

I grinned. "You seriously shouldn't call me that. I don't think you're in any shape to duel Zack."

He chuckled and then winced as he coughed. If Dathan was nearly indestructible, then his face wasn't the only thing wrecked. I braced myself for more.

Picking up speed, I tossed a mass of steel, some wood planks and more drywall over my shoulder, then brushed away more dirt. His raw neck and dislocated shoulders came into view, then his hips and finally his mangled legs. I wondered if there was any part of him that wasn't broken.

"What do you say we get out of here?" I asked, my eyes pooling.

"Might prove a little painful to do on my own. While I've been lying here unable to move, my bones may have healed incorrectly."

"Autumn, we can take it from here." A few feet away, Kayla hitched a thumb, indicating for me to go.

Once I reached the edges of the canyon, Joseph and Kayla went in with a stretcher. Zack draped an arm around my waist. "He's getting a slide this time on the 'sugar' crap. But only because he saved our asses," Zack whispered in my ear.

Havers sidled up next to us and peered over at Dathan. "While you were excavating, we were doing the same and got access into the compound through the skylight. The top floor is intact and any medical equipment should be functional. Dathan can rest in the chapel."

"If it's intact, how did you gain access into the areas we sealed off?" I asked.

Havers snorted. "Who do you think you're talking to? Besides, I had your dad with me for the new codes."

"Right," I said, trying to shake the stupidity from my brain. What I wouldn't give to be able to nap. "Was anyone able to access the parking area?"

"Not yet. We got into some portions of the second floor to determine what parts of the third floor haven't been compromised."

"And?" I raised a brow, willing Havers to give it up.

"Research area, offices and the security area will need some reinforcements before they're safe to walk on," he replied.

"Which means we can use the kitchen." I almost smiled, but then thought about Ivan and Valerie. We needed to find the rest of Natasha's people. But at the moment, my first concern was Dathan. I said goodbye to Havers and followed Joseph and Kayla, hovering until they had Dathan situated in the chapel.

"You won't want to watch this." Kayla ushered me out of the room and followed me into the hallway. "But stay on hand in case we need your help," she ordered and then closed the door in my face. I waited outside the chapel, listening to Dathan's moans and howls as they re-broke his limbs and set them properly. I didn't even want to imagine going through that.

By the time the screams subsided, Zack had returned with blood bags. "Found these in the kitchen. Give them to Dathan and I'll be back in a while to check on you."

"Of course." I ran my fingers through his thick dark hair and stretched up to kiss him.

As soon as Zack disappeared around the corner, Dathan called out to me. "Hey, sugar? Would you come in, please?"

As I let myself into the chapel, Joseph and Kayla exited and I closed the door after them. Although Dathan's skin was blotchy and puckered, no bone protruded from his cheek anymore. "What's on your mind?"

"Ulric was aware of this place, which means so are the men who took Natasha. And most likely Mortimer. It's not safe here. As soon as we possibly can, we'll all go back to my palace while your mother and I convalesce."

I bit my lip, mulling over his idea. "Your palace is only about forty minutes from my house. So...."

"We can't separate." Dathan sliced his hand horizontally through the air, signaling that there was no point in arguing with him. "You, Zack and the rest are coming with me."

"I'll talk to the others about that." I waved and slipped out the chapel door.

My dad met me in the hallway. "They're still excavating where you found Dathan, trying to get to the parking structure through the park. Came across a few shape-shifters." His gaze plummeted to the floor.

"Dead?" My eyes stung and a whimper escaped me.

My dad lifted a shoulder. "Blown apart by the bomb. But they were already dead before the explosion. Clean cuts at the neck. We'll find some alive though, I'm sure of it."

Which meant those bodies weren't Egon, Sean, Yvonne or the others since they had been alive and fighting us before the bomb went off. At least there was that. I sniffed and wiped my cheek. "Have you seen any of Natasha's guards?"

"I didn't, no. But some of the other bodies, well, you can't tell who they are." My dad's jaw tightened.

I didn't expect much. Natasha's guards may not have gotten far enough away. And I'd already figured that Ulric probably would've killed the younger, weaker shape-shifters since they wouldn't have been useful against us. And he wouldn't go out of his way to paralyze them when killing was more efficient. I forced down the lump in my throat. "What if Mortimer's men come back? We need to get out of here."

"They won't. They're all with King Mortimer," my dad growled, "waiting for us to rescue Natasha."

"If I were Mortimer, I'd keep plenty of men with me at the palace to hold the fort," I said. "But I'd also send men to hunt us, just in case we decided to cut our losses and not rescue her."

My dad shook his head. "He knows I'll come for her."

I gripped his arm. "He also won't take the chance that she talks you into not coming after her. Not that you'd leave her there, but that's totally what he'd do. He might expect everyone else to have the same heartless mentality."

His brows arched up in surprise. "My clever girl. You've had to grow up too fast." A sad smile touched his lips. "I'll talk to Renzo and bounce this off him."

I dashed down the hallway and found Zack in the cafeteria, standing in front of the fridge eyeing a blood bag in his hand. "Hungry?" I asked.

"Always." He tossed the blood bag back into the fridge. "But I can't do blood. We'll be descending on the wolves soon and I probably shouldn't smell like a vampire. As it is, the blood I've already consumed will take a while to lose its effect on my scent."

"Right." And I'd continue to abstain from meat so I could pass as human. "Smart."

He grazed a knuckle along my cheek, his other hand gripping the waist of my T-shirt. "Tired?"

"Exhausted. Dathan says we need to leave as soon as we can. My dad's talking to Renzo now, coordinating."

"We still have to find everyone, make sure there isn't anyone left who can be saved." He threw his head back and groaned. "I'm starving."

"Food I can handle. Go. I'll bring you something in a few minutes." I reached up on my toes and pressed my lips against his. "Maybe we can rest wherever we end up. Hang in there."

Zack's throat rumbled as he pulled me against him. "Hanging on is easy, so long as you're with me."

And to think that once we had alone time, I could do all the things with Zack that normal couples did. Except that I couldn't. Because he still believed mixing species would hurt us. And I couldn't tell him, otherwise I'd betray my mom. The next several weeks or months were sure to drag on. For now, I just had to get through the debris and bodies.

CHAPTER TWENTY
———— Autumn ————

HOURS LATER, THEY'D removed enough of the rubble to sort through the bodies in the parking structure. Zack wouldn't let me help. I didn't fight him on it, too grateful not to have to clutter my brain with the gruesome sights. Renzo and Zack spent a considerable amount of time examining each head for any resemblance to anyone they knew.

I occupied myself being nursemaid to both Dathan and my mom, while also running around with my dad doing an inspection of the sleeping quarters. As we moved through each room, we checked it for bodies, as well as functionality. We made a list of damages. As we encountered a handful of the shape-shifters who'd survived, we patched them up as best we could, fed them and took them to the theater to heal.

My dad surveyed the research room. "What a mess."

"All that technology lost." My throat swelled. "Years of hard work."

"They're good at keeping records and making sure the information is backed up. And we have Havers."

"Yeah," I said, as we backed out of the room.

My dad paused to listen to a voice in his head, then patted my back. "Renzo just told me they found Egon, Sean, Yvonne and a few of the others. Broken and battered but once they've eaten, it'll probably only be a few hours before they've healed enough to take over. We can depend on them to make sure every inch is covered and everyone is rescued. Let's see if we can salvage any of our belongings and get packed."

All my breath expelled in relief. They had to feel bad for attacking us, and Egon would probably forever torture himself for allowing Ulric inside. Hopefully, in time they'd realize it wasn't their fault.

† † †

Zack and me, my parents, Renzo and Dathan, plus five other vampires—with room to spare—boarded Cedric's private jet. As we cruised down the dirt road before liftoff, the bumps jostled me. I glanced out the window to see the backhoe running and other shape-shifters moving debris by hand. And then we were in the air.

Keeping his promise to help Sean, Dathan had huddled with Sean before we left to plan out the next couple weeks. Sean agreed to consult him when needed and then Dathan extracted a promise that they wouldn't try to rescue Natasha without our help. Dathan didn't need to force the issue. Though their first priority was to retrieve their queen, they wanted to be smart about it. Their best chance at a rescue mission was to wait until everyone was healed and ready for battle.

Zack and I snuggled in the corner of the jet and managed a few minutes of sleep. When we descended toward Van Nuys airport, I yawned and stretched against Zack. "Hey, did you guys decide where we're going?"

"No way can we allow our king to convalesce some place without decent security." Kayla lifted her chin in challenge.

"Kayla is right," my mom said. "King Cedric can keep him safer."

"Damn straight we can," Joseph said in a tone that dared us to argue. "Which is why you guys are coming with us too. You're important to our king. Therefore, you're important to us. Conversation over."

Not like any of us would've argued anyway. But, oh, how I would've loved to go home and get some clothes that I hadn't already been wearing the last several weeks.

"We have no choice but to go to the palace." My mom's mouth curved down. "As much as I'd love to be in my own home again."

"You two aren't sharing a room." My dad sent Zack a dark look. "If His Majesty can't spare an extra room, then one of us or Renzo will bunk with you guys."

Having Renzo or either of my parents sleep in the same room with Zack and me had certainly worked to keep our hormones in check. All the more reason to rush my mom and Dathan's recovery so we could descend upon the werewolf king and no longer have to hide or cower. The sooner we got started, the better. And then Zack and I could truly be together. That was something worth fighting for.

"They've been sharing a room for months, Quentin," Dathan said as the jet eased to a stop on the runaway.

My dad's head snapped to me. "What?"

I winced. "Thanks so much, Dathan. Not sure why we dug you out of the rubble."

Joseph opened the door and motioned us out of the plane toward three waiting limos. Wanting nothing more than to escape that topic, I bailed. My mom and Dathan were still weak and we hadn't come all this way to be ambushed. I flanked my mom while my dad covered her other side. Zack and Renzo shielded Dathan as he shuffled toward the long black car. Kayla, Joseph and the other three circled us.

On the way to the vampire palace, I snuggled against Zack and dozed off, rousing as we turned up the long driveway.

"Welcome home," King Cedric greeted us as we exited the limo.

The vampires helped us with our luggage and Cedric ushered us up to his suite. "I hope you don't mind but I want to keep you all close by."

"Reminds me of old times," I said with a sigh. Sure, I was honored Cedric would make sure we were all safe, but I'd had enough of being crowded with so little privacy.

Dathan headed up the stairs and I followed. He'd have to unpack and needed to conserve his strength. I'd do that for him. He blocked me at the doorway to his room. "I'm not as weak as you may think. I'm merely reserving my strength to promote healing."

I ignored him, swooping and snatching the bag out of his hand. "Good. So save your strength while I unpack for you."

"I have people who will do that for me. Leave the bags there." But Dathan didn't object while I steered him to his room and unzipped his bags, laying some items in drawers and hanging his shirts in the closet. "I'll be fine," he said after I finished.

"If you need anything, call one of us. I want you conserving your energy." I raised my brows in warning then made my way back to Cedric's office where everyone had gathered. By their grave expressions, something bad had gone down. I met all five sets of eyes. "What did I miss?"

"Zack volunteered to join the werewolves and make himself available to King Mortimer." My mom's eyes were uncharacteristically shiny.

"You're joking." I glanced at Zack but he avoided making eye contact with me. My stomach bottomed out.

Cedric sighed. "Terrible idea."

"Ridiculous. Doesn't merit even a second of our consideration," Renzo growled, glaring at his son.

My mouth dropped open and I tried to speak but only one thought echoed through my brain. Once Zack left, I might never see him again. I forced my lips to move. "That's the stupidest thing ever. Nothing is worth being alone there and unprotected."

"Well said, Autumn." Renzo scowled at Zack. "When we infiltrate Mortimer's palace, it will be painstakingly planned and we'll do it together as a group."

"However..." Dathan raised an index finger as he dragged himself through the doorway and into the office, then sunk to the couch. "As a new recruit, Zack will be treated decently enough, as long as they believe he's one of them. No one will suspect he's there to study the layout and take notes on people—who's who and their routines. By the time we get there, he'll have all the information we need to attack and win. Possibly even Natasha's location. If he's already been there a while, they'll have no reason to suspect he's with us."

It was a brilliant plan, in theory. Yet the worst one I'd ever heard. "No, Zack. Hell, no. We can't risk anything happening to you. This isn't just your responsibility. It's all of ours."

"Okay, okay." My dad waved to get our attention. "None of us want Zack to go anywhere. But..." He risked a glance at me and my stomach lurched.

Please don't, Dad. I can't lose him.

You won't. If I believed he'd be in any real danger, I'd never allow it. My dad refocused on the others. "I spent time with King Mortimer ages ago and I know how they operate. The risk is minimal for a rookie. They have no reason to assume he's there for any other reason than to serve his king. They'll treat him like a newbie, educate him, train him. So long as he's careful and doesn't take any chances—which will only happen if he talks too much—they'll never suspect him."

My eyes burned with unshed tears. "We agreed to stick together. We need to get Natasha out of there, but we can't sacrifice one person for another."

"Autumn." Zack reached for me but then backed away. "I'm not surrendering to the enemy. They'll think I'm their friend, so there's no sacrifice. And this isn't just for Natasha. It's for every shape-shifter out there who lost his life too early, every shifter who slaved for decades, only for their existence to end in a cruel and senseless death. It's for you and me, so we can be together without fear."

And Zack was the only one who could do it since the werewolves were already aware of Renzo as a traitor. Having Zack spying on the werewolves could mean the difference in failing and Natasha dying, or succeeding and winning our freedom. Still, I hated it.

"They'll smell the vampire on him and know something is up." Even if they still wanted to go through with the plan days from now, that would give me several more days with Zack. And I'd know he was alive and well.

My dad shook his head, sending me a sympathetic look. "I'm sorry, sweetheart, but he passes the sniff test. Almost anyway."

No argument there. I'd never noticed any vampire smell on him unless he'd had blood very recently.

Zack averted my gaze. "If anyone gets close enough to me and comments, I'll tell them I encountered a newbie vampire along the way, and I was hungry."

"They'll know who Zack is." I searched their faces, my eyes pleading for them to see reason. "Ulric had infiltrated the minds of the shape-shifters. He had to know about Zack long before he set his plan in motion. He would've relayed everything about us to his king."

"Which is why he'll have a new identity. His papers will be ready shortly." Cedric gave me an apologetic look. "And no one outside this room will know Zack left to join the werewolves. We can't risk any spies informing Mortimer. Everyone, including my people, will think you and he broke up, and he's with his family."

More pretending we're not together. I could hardly wait. But as much as I loathed every part of the plan, this wasn't a battle I could win, not when I was grossly outnumbered. I'd failed. My throat ached. "When are you leaving?"

"Tonight, after I visit with Trevor and Aunt Cara."

The already tense muscles in my shoulders began cramping. "Why so soon? You haven't even caught up on sleep." Not even tomorrow would be sufficient time to say goodbye.

"Because Dathan and I will be ready for battle in about a month," my mom answered, caressing my cheeks with her palms. "Zack needs every second of that month to do what he needs to do. He has all day today to rest before driving out."

Which meant that I wouldn't even get the day with Zack. Because he'd be sleeping instead of spending that time with me. Frustration smothered me like plastic wrap.

"Sweetheart, this can't be easy for you. But Zack has only a few weeks to absorb so much in order to make it possible for us to rescue Natasha and defeat Mortimer." She stroked my arm. "Not much time, Autumn. We need to make every moment count."

"Especially since it's not a quick drive there," my dad added. "It's in Glendale."

Hope sprung within me. "That's a twenty minute drive. He can leave in the morning and get there in time for breakfast."

Dathan winced. "Glendale, *Utah*. Seven or eight hour drive, depending on the length of his stops. If Zack leaves by midnight, he'll arrive first thing in the morning. Each hour Natasha is alone and suffering..." Dathan's jaw clenched. "The sooner Zack gets there, the sooner he can contact her and she'll know she's not alone, that help is on the way."

My heart pounded and my ears roared. I flew past the door, raced down the hallway and down the stairs, then headed outside through the back. I didn't have much time to say goodbye to Zack, but I couldn't speak to anyone. Not even him. Not yet.

Slouching on the cement bench beside the flowerbed, I stared up at the sky. Just months ago, I'd been experimenting with my superhuman abilities, wondering what I was and why I had all these crazy powers. Zack had been practically a stranger, just some smokin' hot guy who'd been rude to me. And now, we were on the brink of war, about to fight for our own lives as well as all shape-shifters. The magnitude of what we'd taken on hit me like a club and my chest squeezed.

"I want to spend time with my family under different circumstances other than my mom's funeral. I may not have another chance for a while." Zack slipped beside me, gently sliding an arm around my waist. "I want you to come with me."

I sniffed and reached deep down inside myself for a smile to offer. Zack didn't want to join King Mortimer any more than I did. He was doing it to help rescue Natasha, and possibly help my species. His willingness to go on this solitary mission made me love him even more. "Sure. I'd like to see your family. But I think we'd better rehearse our story first, make sure we have everything straight."

"Any ideas?" His fingertips glided up my back.

"We'll tell them my mom and dad are considering another job out of town but they want to scope the place out first, make sure the situation will work for them. And they invited us to come along. How could you resist a free trip?"

"And why do I need the Jeep?"

Crap, yeah, he'd need a car to drive to Utah. How would we explain that? "Actually, I won't be needing the Mustang since they'll never let me go anywhere alone and Dathan will probably want to travel in something bigger."

He leaned his head against mine. Silence lengthened and I hated the uncomfortableness of it. But I wouldn't break it. Because once someone spoke, that meant progression. And progression meant taking the next step, and soon after Zack would be gone. For now, I wanted to pretend Zack wasn't going anywhere.

"I should get to bed. I need to sleep as much as possible to drive all night."

Except for the nap on the jet and a few moments of rest in the limo, we hadn't slept since the day before the explosion. Zack couldn't drive straight through without stopping. And stopping for breaks would increase his chances of running into another werewolf. Since that species had a reputation for having no compassion, if Zack were spotted, he might not make it to Mortimer. He had no choice but to catch a few hours here.

And my dad had already forbidden us to share a room.

When we got to Cedric's suite, I palmed the panel and the lock clicked. Nice that they hadn't programmed us out. When we stepped inside, five sets of eyes found us.

Dathan leaned a hip against Cedric's desk. "You can sleep in my room."

"Which is exactly where *you* should be," Cedric said, jabbing a finger in Dathan's direction. "You need to rest and heal too."

"I will. Later." Dathan pointed Zack toward the bedroom. "Go."

Zack dragged me toward Dathan's room. Yeah, as if my dad was going to let me sleep in there with Zack. I glanced over my shoulder to see my dad rising from the sofa, his shoulders rigid, hands balling into fists.

But why should I allow my dad to have any say about my love life? *Don't, Dad.* I sent him a gentle but determined look. *I'm over eighteen. I won't let you waste these last moments I have with Zack.* I disappeared into Dathan's room.

Zack closed the door then stared at it for a beat. *I think we're in the clear.*

I finally had Zack to myself. *This room isn't soundproof,* I reminded him. *They'll hear every creak of the bed, rustling of clothes. We can barely move without them knowing.*

He lowered his mouth to mine and kept it there as he cupped my face with his palms. *I have to sleep anyway.*

Yeah, he did. I resigned myself to cuddling. Though his musky scent and the feel of his warm, rough skin against mine made me want to slip out the window with him and find someplace in the woods with more privacy, I had to resist.

CHAPTER TWENTY-ONE

——— *Zack* ———

I STEERED AUTUMN'S Mustang over the dirt road then veered left and parked under the cover of a cluster of trees. A shiver sent goose bumps along my arms as I anticipated our run. I'd gone out with Renzo and Autumn's parents after the explosion, but that felt like days ago. I was so ready to morph.

It had taken some serious talking to convince the others that Autumn and I would be safe by ourselves for a couple hours. I argued that Ulric was dead and his men had left. Any of his men who may have been lurking at the shape-shifter compound couldn't have followed the jet and couldn't have known where we went.

In the end, we compromised. Olivia and Dathan stayed behind at the vampire palace to heal while Quentin and my dad drove with Autumn and me in the Mustang she'd left at the palace weeks ago. Quentin and my dad decided to stay at Autumn's house while we went for a run in the woods, then visited with my family. If either had done otherwise, they'd been super stealthy about it. For all intents and purposes we were alone, the way it used to be—before we met Renzo or the vampires.

As soon as I killed the engine, I exploded from the car, my feet landing with a thud on the dirt and crunching under a branch. Damn. I'd gotten too used to the privacy of the underground park and not having to worry about being quiet. Or being spotted.

Chastising myself for being so noisy, I scanned the area to make sure no one was around. We couldn't allow any humans to catch us morphing. When I didn't see anything, I drew in a lungful of air to check for scents. Nothing. I relaxed. Autumn slammed the car door and she was already turning into a wolf as she galloped deeper into the forest. "Don't bother waiting for me," I muttered.

Don't be so slow, she teased.

I chuckled as I rolled my eyes and shifted into a wolf, then sprinted to catch up to her.

† † †

Refreshed from our run in the nearby woods, we cruised into the driveway of Aunt Cara's house.

I grinned at Autumn. "We're just in time for dinner."

She stared at the door doubtfully. "Don't get too excited. She might not have made enough since she wasn't expecting us."

"We're talking about Aunt Cara who always cooks enough to feed the whole neighborhood." I headed up the path to the familiar yellow house where I supposedly still lived yet hadn't seen in weeks.

"I hope you're right." She paused at the front door. "Maybe we should've called first."

"And in between the time I talked to them and actually arrived, they'd assume I'm staying. And I'm not." We shouldn't have come and given them hope. But what if things turned bad with King Mortimer and my family never saw me again? Aunt Cara had already lost her sister; I couldn't disappear without stopping by one more time.

The sound of laughing from the kitchen warmed me as I opened the front door. God, I'd missed them. Aunt Cara glanced up from the table, gasped and dashed over to me. "Autumn, Zack."

She squeezed me tight and I hugged her back. And then everyone else rushed me. Mac caught me in a bear hug and a split second later, my cousins Patrick and Brian wrapped themselves around my waist. After a long moment, they disbanded and Trevor sidled up to me.

"Good to have you back, man." He reached an arm across my back and leaned in to whisper, "Maya knows your secret."

I caught my jaw before it dropped. My cousin Trevor had been dating Maya, Autumn's best friend, for months. But Autumn and I had been extremely careful. Neither of them could possibly know *the* secret.

"I'm going to steal Zack but we won't be long. I'm not stupid enough to come between Zack and his food." He offered Autumn a smile then shared it with the rest of them. "I'll return him in a minute."

We hustled down the hallway but instead of stopping at his bedroom door, he tugged on my arm and shoved me into the small room that Aunt Cara had set up months ago for Autumn to sleep. He shut the door behind us and darted to the window to make sure it was closed. "Maya knows," he said in a low voice.

I blinked, not sure I wanted an answer to my question. "Knows what?"

Trevor huffed. "Dude, we've been like brothers for years. I figured out your secret months ago."

He couldn't be referring to me being a werewolf. Humans weren't allowed to know about us. If another werewolf suspected a human had that kind of knowledge, the human could be killed. Well, I'd have to show him he was wrong.

"And?" I asked, pretending to be thoroughly mystified.

"I don't have time to play dumb, Zack. As soon as you and Aunt Favianne moved in, you were sneaking out every night. You obviously didn't want to share whatever it was and I was worried. So one night when you slipped out, I was already in the woods up in the highest tree waiting for you. I'd read your dad's books before that, so after I stopped trying to convince myself you couldn't possibly be a werewolf, I remembered how important it was to keep it a secret, even from you. I didn't want you to worry. But... now that Maya saw you turn into a wolf, I can't pretend anymore. So let's fast forward past all the denials and decide what we're going to do about it."

I swallowed. Yeah, didn't seem like I'd be able to convince Trevor of an alternate reality anytime soon. "H-how did Maya see?"

"We were parked in the woods earlier tonight. Lame, yeah. But damn if we can get any privacy around here or her house. We heard a car coming and when we glanced up Autumn's Mustang rolled by. I didn't have to wonder what you were about to do. But Maya had already recognized her car and then Autumn suddenly morphed and it was too late. After you guys ran off, I got Maya calmer and we left."

This was all wrong. I forced my lungs to work, taking long deep breaths. "I don't understand how I didn't hear you guys, catch your scent or something."

Trevor scoffed. "How could you hear anything beyond your own noise? And we never even got out of the car or rolled the windows down, so you wouldn't have smelled us. You didn't see us because I'd driven the Jeep between a couple low-hanging trees. We didn't want to get caught. But we could still see you through the back window."

I groaned. "Where's Maya now?"

"She's in my room. She didn't want me taking her home because she was too freaked out. But she couldn't eat yet and didn't want Aunt Cara noticing something was wrong. I told them she had cramps and she was lying down for a few minutes."

"Maybe Autumn can handle Maya." I chewed the inside of my mouth while I pondered my dilemma.

"About that... dude, did you change Autumn into a werewolf? What the hell?"

"I didn't change anyone. And she's not a werewolf."

Trevor snorted.

"She's a shape-shifter. There's a difference. She can morph into almost anything while I'll only ever be a wolf."

Trevor shook his head. "Whatever. Let's get back out there and then you should send Autumn to my room to talk to Maya."

Autumn had better talk damn good or we were in trouble. Maya too. If she couldn't pretend as well as Trevor, she didn't just risk our lives but hers and Trevor's too.

Trevor slapped me on the back, gave me a nod and exited the room.

Autumn was seated at the table scarfing pasta, making me envious. The pasta smelled incredible. I'd give her a chance to enjoy a bit more before I dropped the bomb.

Not like I had time to fill her in with all the questions hurled at me. My gaze ricocheted around the table while I fired off answers to their questions, carefully avoiding what I'd really been doing all this time. Somehow, I managed to get enough food in my face.

"It's so good to see you." Cara beamed. "Are you going to try to get your job back at the auto shop?"

My smile faded. Here we go... "No, I can't. Actually, I'm leaving tonight."

"My parents invited him on a road trip. My dad's picking up a job in Texas." Autumn cast me a quick glance. "I don't think Zack is ready to return to his old life yet. So we'll probably stay in Texas a few months."

Silence blanketed the table and Aunt Cara pushed her plate away. She rose, rounded the table, then slung her arms around his shoulders and landed a kiss on the top of his head. "Do what you need to do. We'll always be here for you."

"Thank you, Aunt Cara." He reached up to squeeze her hand. "Love you."

She gave him a quick pat and reclaimed her chair. "If nothing else, you'll come back for the food."

You guys were gone so long. What did Trevor have to say? Autumn asked as she tore off a hunk of garlic bread.

I glanced down at her nearly empty plate. *I'll tell you after dinner.*

She froze, peered over at me then loaded the next forkful slower, as if she was expecting bad news and she wanted to put it off.

When everyone had finished eating, Aunt Cara began cleaning up. I leaped from my chair. "Autumn and I will do that."

She flicked her wrist in the air, waving me off. "You're leaving soon. Enjoy yourself."

Right, I didn't have much time and we still needed to work out what do to with Maya. I swiveled my chair to face Autumn and leaned into her like we were about to have a private conversation. Which we were. *Maya and Trevor were in the woods tonight. They both saw us. Turns out, Trevor has known about me this whole time. But Maya isn't processing this too well. She's in Trevor's room now freaking out.*

I waited for her to answer and when she didn't, I noticed her eyes were pooling. I stroked her arm. *You have to convince her that everything is okay. Make sure she understands how important it is that she keep our secret as well as Trevor did.*

Because if she doesn't, they could die. Autumn's arm trembled beneath my fingertips. *And it would've been my fault because I was sloppy tonight. How could I have been so stupid?*

I can't blame you because I was there and just as stupid. Go talk to her. I angled backward, putting some distance between us, a silent signal for her to get on with it. *She's a smart girl. She can do this.*

I hoped.

CHAPTER TWENTY-TWO

——— *Autumn* ———

I TAPPED ON the door to Trevor's room as a warning, but didn't wait for a reply. The door gave way to reveal Maya sitting on the foot of the bed, staring at the dresser in front of her. Without a word, I sat next to her.

"I guess you're a bit freaked out," I said softly, not wanting to spook her, but also not wanting anyone besides Zack to overhear our conversation.

Seconds ticked by. "Kind of."

"How can I help?"

"I'm pretty much over it, I guess. Mostly, I just have a lot questions." She pivoted toward me and lifted her chin. "For starters, if you have these superhuman abilities, why were you afraid of Daniel?" Seeing my hesitation, she barreled on. "Trevor told me that you two are much stronger than humans and your senses are sharper."

And how the hell did Trevor know all that? Clearly he'd been paying attention while we were too busy underestimating him. "True. If Daniel had been a mere human, I wouldn't have been worried."

Her eyes brightened. "Daniel was a werewolf too?"

"Not at first. Long story, but remember when he disappeared and the rumor spread that he'd been dragged away by a wolf? All true."

Maya slapped her palms to her cheeks. "You're kidding."

"You have no idea how much I wish it was all a joke. The guy who changed him into a werewolf was stalking Zack, so he and I decided we should stick together." I tapped her knee. "And guess what else? Zack and I really weren't a thing back then, even though you never believed me."

She plopped back onto the mattress in a fit of giggles. "That's amazing."

Relief swelled within me that she wasn't flipping out. But this was no joke. "Maya, I need you to understand something. This is important."

She moaned and propped herself up. "But I want to live in a fantasy world and believe that you guys were traipsing across the country these past few weeks and not gone because someone's after you."

"I'm sorry. I wish I could tell you what you want to hear. Listen, Maya..." I paused to make sure she was listening. "You can't talk about this with anyone, not even Trevor. If anyone were to overhear, which is easy with our enhanced senses, they'll kill you. It's forbidden for humans to know we exist."

She mulled that over a moment. "I have so many more questions. Just tell me this: do I have reason to worry about you two?"

Should I lie my ass off to spare her feelings? Or tell her the truth to relieve my own? "We have a lot of protection. Get this." I nudged her with my elbow. "We're buddies with the vampire king."

"Vampires?" She blinked as that sunk in. "Oh, my God. I have to meet one."

"Maybe you will one day. I can't vouch for a lot of them, but if you ever come across a scary vampire named Dathan, he's okay. For now, I need you to promise me that you and Trevor will never speak of this again. Ever. Especially if you think no one can hear you."

"I pinky swear." She held out her little finger and I crossed mine over hers. "Have I met any other werewolves?"

I chuckled, realizing she wasn't going to let up until I gave up a tidbit. "Renzo and Alura."

Maya snorted. "No way."

"Yes way. My dad and Renzo are at my house right now. Waiting for us." I wanted to tell her Favianne was still alive, but I didn't feel like it was my place to give away any vampire secrets. Even Favianne's. Plus, the less Maya knew, the safer she'd be.

"Your dad... I guess that explains why they were always moving from city to city and hovering over you, huh? They were trying to keep you safe from..." She lifted one eyebrow as she stared at me expectantly.

I sighed. "Yes and that's all I can say. I should get back out there and spend some time with the others."

Maya's lip jutted into a pout. "I wish I could keep you a while longer. I've missed you so much."

"Not more than I've missed you. I'll try to call you again soon." As I gave her hope, I realized there wasn't any. Not yet. My parents and the rest of them would never allow me to go anywhere without them, not anytime soon. And if they were around Maya and me for very long, they'd probably figure out she knew something. The farther she stayed from them, the better.

Maya threw her head back and moaned. "My college classes begin next week and I'll only be available at night. I'll be busy studying or slaving over whatever design project I'm working on. But I'll make time for you."

I had no idea how demanding the fashion institute was, but knowing Maya, she'd excel. And that meant she'd stay busy. Good.

"Me too." No matter what happened next or what my future held, I'd find a way to keep my friendship with her.

† † †

Zack's belongings sat near the door, obscene in their abundance. He'd packed nearly everything he owned. Which was understandable. If the werewolves believed he had all his worldly belongings with him and no ties left behind, they'd believe he was starting a new life with them.

I wanted to look away, but I couldn't. Zack was leaving. And if anything went wrong, he could be killed. This could be the last time I saw him.

Zack touched his forehead against mine. *Let's take a quick walk before I go.*

We're not supposed to be out there alone. We're lucky they let us go to the woods earlier and to see your family, I said, knowing we'd already pushed Renzo and my dad's patience. My dad had disappeared into his office upstairs and Renzo was down the hallway on the phone. They'd be pissed if we left without telling them. *We shouldn't be out there by ourselves. I don't want to press our luck.*

I want a few moments alone with you, Zack said, surreptitiously scanning the room. *We won't be far.*

Zack wouldn't ask if it wasn't important, so I nodded. Hand-in-hand, we stepped outside and veered in the opposite direction of his house. Seconds ticked by and neither of us spoke. I wasn't sure if I could get any words past my swollen throat anyway. Several houses down, he slowed to a stop and twirled me until I was facing him. "I need you to know where we stand before I go. It's not fair to you if I don't say anything."

Oh, God. What now? He didn't want me to wait for him?

"Being with you..." He gave a slight shake of his head before continuing. "Since the moment you bumped into me, I've never wanted any other girl. It's always been you, Autumn."

"I feel the same way about you." I held my breath, hoping he wasn't about to tell me that his feelings wouldn't be enough to survive our separation and we should end it now.

"That we can't explore a physical relationship in depth sucks. It's always sucked and it always will."

He planted his hand behind my neck, making it impossible for me to squirm away. "But that couldn't be nearly as bad as being without you."

And I could breathe again. "I concur," I whispered.

"I don't want to be without you, Autumn. Ever. And I couldn't leave here without you knowing..." He paused, slowly exhaling then filling his lungs again. "I'm in love with you. Since you first wore that purple dress, there's been no going back for me. You could be some other creature with all the wrong lady parts and I'd still never get enough of you. I'd still want to be with you. Forever."

So not what I was expecting. I jumped, ready to throw myself at him and he thrust out a palm to stop me. He reached into his pocket and dropped to one knee. "We're young and people might say we don't know what love is. But I know there will never be anyone else for me."

"I feel the same." But why was he kneeling? "Get up. This is weird."

I could hear his heart thrashing beneath his chest. "I was going to wait because... I didn't want to freak you out. But I can't leave without doing this. And maybe not next month and maybe not next year, but someday I hope that you'll agree to... make it legal."

I froze. Make what legal? No way could he be talking about marriage.

Zack opened his hand to reveal a red velvet box. He lifted the lid and a gigantic diamond ring twinkled up at me. "It's a lot to ask, I know. You don't have to answer me. But if you wanted to wear it while I'm gone, that would be okay."

My eyes began leaking and I wiped away tears with my fingertips. "I thought you were going to break up with me. And tell me not to wait for you." A sob snuck out which made the tears more plentiful. I sniffed and averted my face in an effort to compose myself. And maybe I could get a moment to say something more profound.

"D-do you want to wear it? Or would that be too weird?"

I glanced at the ring again. I'd never seen that kind of filigree and the metal didn't look smooth and polished like modern rings. Although the rock was the biggest diamond I'd ever seen in real life, the ring was far from perfect, as if someone lovingly created it by hand without the aid of modern technology.

I loved it.

I gave him a watery laugh, plucking the ring from the box and shoving it past my knuckle. "I would be honored to wear your ring, Zack De Luca."

Zack pulled me into a hug and I buried my nose in his neck, wrapped my arms around his waist and pressed as close to him as I possibly could. "I love you. More than anyone or anything."

† † †

Zack drove away ten minutes later. We all waved to him from the curb, staring down the street until the Mustang turned the corner and disappeared. Renzo draped an arm around my shoulder and guided me away. "He'll check in hourly. He'll be fine. We'll get through this."

Renzo believed we'd get through it, but I wasn't as sure. Zack and I hadn't been apart in months, not for more than a few hours at a time. Already, withdrawals were creeping up on me and worry blanketed me.

We had so much to accomplish these next few months. Zack had to stay undercover, we needed to rescue Natasha, dethrone Mortimer and free my species. I vowed to keep the faith that Zack and I would survive this—that we all would—and we could be together again soon.

THE END

If you enjoyed this book, please recommend it to friends, reader's groups and discussion boards or tell others how much you enjoyed it by reviewing it on Amazon, GoodReads or your own site.
Thank you and happy reading!

)

BOOKS IN THE SHAPES OF AUTUMN SERIES:

Thrown to the Wolves: The Legend of Hannah & Eli
(Shapes of Autumn, prequel)

My Wolf's Bane (Shapes of Autumn, book one)

Wolves at the Door (Shapes of Autumn, book two)

Dead Wolf Walking (Shapes of Autumn, book three)

The Dark Wolf (Shapes of Autumn, book four)

Lord of the Wolves (Shapes of Autumn, book five)

† † †

For updates on releases, please visit
www.VERONICABLADE.com

SHAPES OF AUTUMN SERIES

Different species.
Mortal enemies.
It'll never work,
but they'll die trying.

*Thrown to the Wolves:
The Legend of Hannah
& Eli* (prequel)

My Wolf's Bane
(book one)

Wolves at the Door
(book two)

Dead Wolf Walking
(book three)

The Dark Wolf
(book four)

Lord of the Wolves
(book five)

More Titles by Veronica Blade

A newbie witch enlists help from the scrumptious school bad-boy to make her life and death choice between two battling covens.

A Cinderella who spends her nights as a wolf. A prince with a taste for blood.

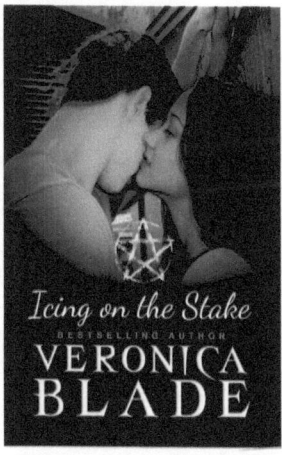

Sofia lays her hard-won anonymity on the line by saving the most popular boy in school. Worse, she's been exposed to the vampire hunters who attacked him.

The witch queen must make the impossible choice between abandoning the throne and her people, or spending eternity with the man she loves.

More Titles by Veronica Blade

Should a woman who's unable to forget her first love give "happily ever after" one more try?

When good-girl Maddie switches places with her famous bad-girl twin Jackie, she has some pretty high stilettos to fill.

When Hunter realizes he botched the annulment of his marriage to his longtime friend, he must decide if she and their marriage are worth fighting for.

A micro trilogy including Single-Handed, Singled Out (book two) & Single-minded (book three).

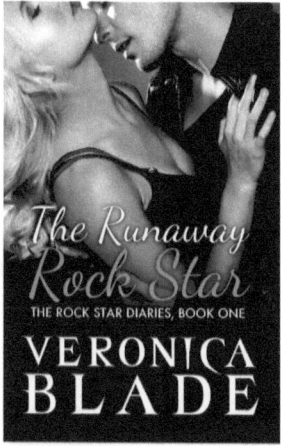

ABOUT VERONICA BLADE

VERONICA BLADE LIVES near Carson City, Nevada with her husband and furbabies but also spends a lot of time in southern California. She writes sweet romances to live vicariously through her characters. Except her heroes and heroines lead far more interesting lives—and they are always way hotter.

)

You can visit Veronica Blade on Facebook, check out her website at VeronicaBlade.com or follow her on Twitter @VeronicaBlade. You can even e-mail her at veronica@veronicablade.com. She loves hearing from readers!

www.ingramcontent.com/pod-product-compliance
Lightning Source LLC
Chambersburg PA
CBHW030118180626
46812CB00002B/473